ILLUMINATION

Prescriptions for Dealing with Three Blind Mice:
Mental Illness, Miseducation and Poverty

———————

Dr. James E. Savage, Jr.
Dr. Catherine I. Williams

STEPS Publishing

Research and Interior Design by Janaye Jordan
Administrative Assistance by Lydia Wall

Cover Design by Kandice Thompson
Editing by Harristeen Barnes

Printed by STEPS Publishing

First published by STEPS Publishing and the Institute for Life Enrichment (ILE) on: 12/17/2020

ISBN: 978-0-9987455-6-5

Printed in the United States of America

Scriptures marked KJV are taken from the KING JAMES VERSION (KJV): KING JAMES VERSION, public domain.

Dr. Savage is an accomplished and respected clinical psychologist with a diverse background, and Dr. Catherine Williams is an esteemed educator, administrator, community organizer and training specialist. Together they have written a powerful contribution to understanding the damaging and corrosive effects of mental illness in the Black community. Their book, *Illumination,* is lucid and insightful, describing how America's "original sin" of racism has largely been ignored as a contributing nemesis in the pathologies that steal, kill, and destroy much of black social and cultural life. They use an unconventional style as the background to disseminate well researched and very relevant facts pertaining to mental illness, miseducation and poverty. What is singularly important about this book is how they creatively weave so many details of the way mental illness impacts nearly every aspect of society. This book is well written and easy to follow. Although the information is top shelf, the way it is presented is easy to reach. I recommend *Illumination,* to every current and future clinical worker and educator as a valuable resource in seeing into the tangled, unsettling mind and behaviors impacted by mental illness. If you have any interaction with Black people or the Black community, you would do yourself a great dis-service by ignoring this book.

Freddie I. Barnes, Clinical Chaplain II, D.Min, M.Div, BA.

Illumination presents a broad-gauged analysis and solution-driven book that all persons seeking solutions to our societal issues of mental illness, miseducation and poverty should read. Dr. James E. Savage and Dr. Catherine I. Williams put America on the couch. Exploring the causes of societal dysfunction in America; the authors call for some bold approaches designed to improve the lives of the downtrodden. The authors are sensitive to current oppositions to effective government programs, and they recognize the importance of contributions from institutions such as family, churches and voluntary associations. As a journalist who covered urban America since the assassination of Dr. King, I recommend this seminal document for all concerned Americans.

Claude L. Matthews, Attorney and Former NBC Nightly News Producer

Illumination: Prescriptions for Dealing with Three Blind Mice: Mental Illness, Miseducation and Poverty is the merging of spiritual and intellectual energetic resources by two scholars/practitioners - Drs. James E. Savage, Jr. and Catherine I. Williams. It is a fictional, historical, psychological work that centers on the traumatic and residual effects of oppression of Africans in the diaspora. The authors highlight the economic, social, psychological, and spiritual deprivation of people. Aforementioned is authenticated through storytelling as to how Africa was underdeveloped and occupied by Europeans. Savage and Williams present their documentations as activities in "Nommo." The book is partitioned into five parts: The Story Unfolds; Mental Illness; Miseducation; Poverty; and Illumination. The authors' straightforward and inviting approach to this work is notably realistic as a useful strategic tool, and it is exciting. Not only is *Illumination: Prescriptions for Dealing with Three Blind Mice: Mental Illness, Miseducation and Poverty* stimulating and energetic for those in the academy, but it is as appealing to all who come within reachable distances. It is the type of book that should never be allowed to lie on the bookshelf and collect cobwebs. By the way, there is an astonishing compilation, and resource directory included. Don't take my word. Read it for yourself!

O.D. Alexander, PhD, University Librarian, Millennia Atlantic University

This book is dedicated to our parents who instilled values, nurtured us and gave us wisdom and love throughout life's journey: James E. Savage Sr. and the late Thelma Savage; the late Edward V. and Katie M. Williams; surrogate mother, Evelyn V. Williams, and to our family members and colleagues.

This book is also dedicated to past and current clients, participants in various workshops, and everyone laboring to improve the lives and welfare of families and communities throughout the world.

Acknowledgements

To the Creator for His many blessings, gifts and for "ordering our steps." We wish to thank Janaye Jordan, our development editor, for research, dedication and commitment. Special thanks to our dedicated administrative assistant, Lydia Wall; Harristeen Barnes of Divine Touch Proofreading; Kandice Thompson for the cover and illustrations; and Belinda Wyche for the poem, "Illumination".

Table of Contents

Introduction

Illumination is a psychological and empowerment novel which is a blend of fiction and non-fiction used to analyze and synthesize the authors' observations of human systems which led them to conclude that there are negative impacting forces robbing African people in America and throughout the diaspora of optimum human functioning. These negative forces are systemic manifestations that lead to many of us living in darkness, as a blinded people, sightless, to find our way out of the quagmire of debilitating entanglements of racist driven mental illness, miseducation and poverty.

The focus of this novel is the historical, progressive and current interplay of mental illness, miseducation and poverty that lead to incongruence in the lives of African Americans. We recognize that other African people are subject to similar challenges. These are forces that keep us from building healthy immediate living spaces, local communities, powerful families and illuminated children.

Dr. Johnson, a central figure in this book, and his family would gather at his home to tell the children how there are many stories of our mother country, Africa, and how it was invaded, pillaged, plundered and occupied by European countries whose racist intentions were to subjugate African natives and rape them of their natural resources, creations and knowledge. Miseducation of black people in Africa started when depositories of knowledge were destroyed, and European cultural norms supplanted those of Africans. This led to the Atlantic Slave Trade and what has become known as the diabolical Maafa. The authors remember someone telling them that Don Ho, a singer and musician, who was born in Honolulu, Hawaii, once said that evangelists came to Hawaii with bibles and told the natives to close their eyes, kneel and pray. When they opened their eyes, all their land was gone! This blinding scenario not only played out in Hawaii but also throughout Africa and continues today.

The story of the three blind mice is applicable in the Americas, especially in the United States. We see mental illness, miseducation and poverty affecting our people daily. In our enslavement, miseducation was central to maintain us as chattel. Concurring with the rape of our minds were diagnoses that were described in Sillen and Thomas' book *Racism in Psychiatry* (e.g., Drapetomania and Africanus Aethiopicus). Poverty was a constant for slaves since they could not own any means of production and consume only what the slave owners provided. This book will elucidate how the three blind mice of mental illness, miseducation and poverty, driven by racism, have impacted black lives historically and what we can do to move from "darkness to marvelous light," so that our children, their children, and their children's children can be illuminated—moving from blindness to sight.

In order to come out of the darkness, we must have community control of our local institutions. They must provide optimum conditions for black families and black children. Power must reside with the people so that they can coordinate activities, programs, structures and mental health healing.

Illumination will help to change mental illness to psychological wellness; miseducation to enlightenment; and poverty to economic sufficiency. In other words, illumination will help to eradicate the three blind mice.

PART I
The Story Unfolds *

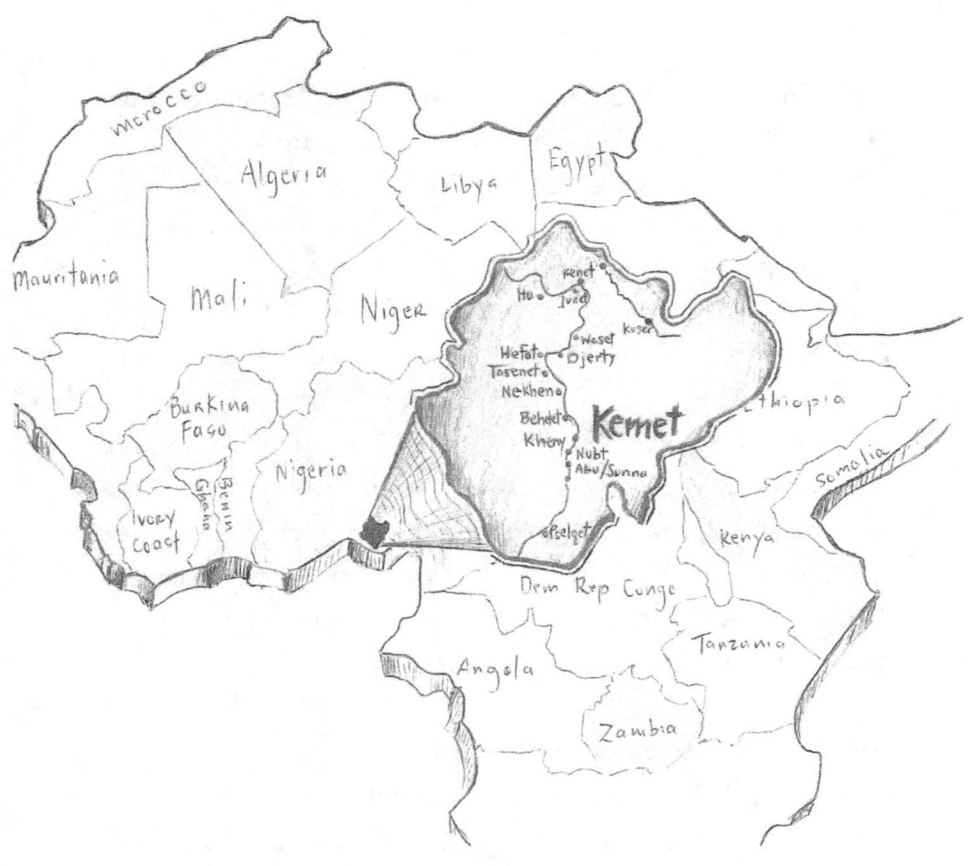

* The above illustration was created based on maps in Africa
(www.criticxxtreme.wordpress.com) and Kemet (www.oocities.org)

The Johnson Family

Our story begins with Grandma, Lucille Johnson, a 69-year-old widow, her family (i.e., her three grandchildren, her brother John, and his wife Mildred). The children need to understand some African history and how it relates to their lives and the world today.

GRANDMA JOHNSON is a loving, devoted and hardworking woman; she is trustworthy, supportive of her family, a great blessing to others and fears the Lord. She is known for standing up for the defenseless and helping her neighbors and friends. After the death of her husband, almost 20 years ago, she developed a much closer relationship with her 49-year-old brother, John, because her sister Anne, a military wife, moved with her husband to Germany when he retired from the United States Army.

Grandma Johnson earns her living as a cook at a hotel and supplements her income with her husband's pension. She is also a seamstress making clothes or altering them from her home. She manages her resources well and lives modestly in a densely populated urban community. Grandma Johnson's house is tucked away behind public housing, just about four blocks from the neighborhood market and the laundromat. The bus stop is a couple of houses down from hers—something she is thankful for, otherwise, she'd have to walk a mile and cross two busy intersections to get to work every day.

Her neighbors are kind but nosey, especially Ms. Doris next door, affectionately known as the Candy Lady of the neighborhood. Grandma Johnson is often left to sweep up candy wrappers and broken lollipop sticks every morning before work. After fifteen years, she welcomes the chore, and it has become part of a morning ritual she's created, tidying the porch and humming her favorite hymns. Plus, the porch was where Grandma Johnson's husband spent most of his time, rocking in his favorite chair and shelling his roasted peanuts. That was his porch, the reason he bought the house, and she couldn't imagine sweeping any other porch after he died. So she kept the house and didn't mind Ms. Doris and the neighborhood kids.

Grandma Johnson's home is quaint, yet large enough for her lifestyle. She keeps it clean and dedicates her Saturday mornings to sweeping the hardwood floors, dusting the shelves and vacuuming each bedroom. Her favorite room is the sewing room, a small converted bedroom on the west side of the house. In the right corner sits an oak table made by her husband, and, on it, her sewing machine—her prized possession.

Another bedroom contains two small beds and a dresser. Grandma Johnson's room, although equally unimpressive, is comfortable and modestly decorated. Twenty minutes in the morning and twenty in the evening each day are spent in her prayer closet, thanking God for her sustenance, health and sanity.

Grandma Johnson has one child, Sabrina, who is 36. Sabrina has three children: a daughter, Jeannie (six years old); a daughter, Sandra (11 years old); and a son, Keith (13 years old). Grandma Johnson dearly loves Sabrina and her grandchildren. Before things went crazy with Sabrina and her husband, Grandma Johnson enjoyed the quality time that she spent with them on the weekends, and she was delighted to keep the children as often as she could. Unfortunately, Sabrina married a man named Charlie, and the marriage would wreak havoc for her life, her children and Grandma Johnson.

CHARLIE is Sabrina's husband and Grandma Johnson's son-in-law. He is the youngest of twelve children who lived in a public housing project in a predominantly black area of a big city. His mother was a domestic worker and his father was an alcoholic who beat his mother and abused him and his siblings. One day, like a thief in the night, Charlie's father left and his mom had to raise them all by herself.

Charlie attended public school, but spent most of his time skipping classes and hanging out with guys on the corner and at the mall. When he was in high school struggling, he dreamed about how he was going to earn a living and make money. Instead of finishing high school, he decided to do something that he thought was easier and more lucrative. So, he dropped out of high school and started to help his neighbor, Mr. Morris, cleaning office buildings, the recreation center and some private homes.

Mr. Morris taught Charlie everything that he knew about the janitorial business. He trusted him and eventually allowed him to work solo on Friday and Saturday nights. He paid Charlie more than the $7.25 minimum wage and frequently gave him extra money. Mr. Morris taught him to value what he called "the almighty dollar."

Charlie was a handsome, sharp dresser; he always had money, and he even had a car while the other fellows his age were still in high school. Charlie was popular, had a gift of gab, and could finesse people. He emulated Mr. Morris who was as smooth as silk and a ladies man. The two of them were "thick as thieves."

One night, Mr. Morris' wife was looking for him to let him know that a relative had been in a car accident and rushed to the emergency room. Charlie went across town to the building where Mr. Morris was working. To his surprise, he saw three men giving Mr. Morris money as he gave them bundles of something wrapped in plastic. He waved a gun and said, "Don't f- - k with my money, and meet me back here tomorrow night." Charlie was shocked but managed to say, "Cuse me Mr. Morris. I just came to bring you a message from your wife." Mr. Morris immediately dismissed the men and said, "Come on in son. Grab a chair and sit down. I've been planning to let you in on something and hadn't gotten around to it. Now's the time!"

Mr. Morris poured and snorted a line of coke as he explained how he really made his money. The janitorial business was a front that allowed him to be away from home at night and run his drug business without any suspicion from his wife, neighbors, and friends. He swore Charlie to secrecy, promised to make him a partner, and vowed to kill him if he ever ran his mouth or messed up his money. He also warned Charlie not to use drugs, only sell them—nothing and no one was sacred, but the dollar! Needless to say, Charlie was excited and ready to be "the Man"—just like Mr. Morris.

At age 15, Charlie became the neighborhood "pusher-man"—selling drugs. He made a lot of money and he looked out for his family by paying bills, buying groceries and giving his brothers and sisters whatever they needed for school, clothes and fun. Charlie was "the man"—on top of his game as a big-time drug dealer!

His drug business grew by leaps and bounds from Baltimore to Delaware and to Philadelphia. The more money Charlie made, the more he wanted, and he would stop at nothing to be on top, to become one of the drug kings of the East Coast. The road to the top was a costly one that he never thought about.

Along the way, he met Sabrina—a lovely girl, clean cut, from a solid middle class working family. She was the apple of Grandma Johnson's eye, the beat of her heart.

SABRINA is Grandma Johnson's only child. Grandma and her husband worked hard for Sabrina to grow up in a good home. And she did. Sabrina respected her parents, always took their advice, and always made her curfew. "Go to college; get a good job; marry a respectable man," her parents' instructions resounded in her throughout her adolescence like the lyrics of a song she couldn't shake. And she was determined to do all of those things and to make her parents proud.

At age 15, Sabrina decided that she wanted to be a pediatrician after watching her young cousin recover from a bicycle fall. She was there when he sped down the street, hands raised in the air and teasing her that he was a better rider than she was. Speeding beyond control, his bike quickly drifted to the curb, and he plunged into the sidewalk—arms first. He was rushed to the local hospital, and Sabrina went with him. His left arm was broken. The doctor on duty was warm, friendly, and had a magnetic personality. He made her cousin laugh so hard while telling a funny story that he forgot that his limb had just been jammed back into its socket. He immediately eased her cousin's pain and fear. Sabrina wanted to wield the same physical and mental healing power herself. So she decided that she wanted to become a doctor.

Four years of pre-med school was hard, but Sabrina excelled, learning to love late nights and day-old coffee. She maintained strong relationships with her professors and participated in a couple of extra-curricular activities. Her favorite was the Black Student Association (BSA), where she held a leadership position and dedicated her few extra hours to planning meetings and events that took place at the African House on campus.

BSA introduced Sabrina to an aspect of African American culture which she never fully experienced while growing up at home. Her parents were strict and did not tolerate Sabrina hanging out with anyone who did not meet their approval. In high school, she loved to read and study, and she spent a lot of time at the library while the other girls her age were at the skating rink or at each other's houses. Her time spent studying as a recluse was not in vain, as she landed a full-tuition scholarship to a major, predominantly white university and eased in with no problem.

Needless to say, the struggles of Sabrina's BSA friends to get in, stay in, and excel in college were unfamiliar to her, and she eventually realized that she had lived quite a sheltered life. Most of them had to work one or two part- time jobs to afford school, while the others admitted to having to take out massive student loans. Few had help from their families, and most were the first in their families to attend college. She appreciated her friends and gained a lot of insight listening to their stories.

By the time graduation rolled around, Sabrina had been dating Charlie for three months. She decided that four additional years at med school plus another three years in residency would take too long to accomplish, so she happily settled for a decent-paying research position at the university while she mapped out her next steps. All she knew was that they would include Charlie, and she had successfully met her parents' expectations.

Charlie and Sabrina fell in love and got married. They were happily married for 14 years and had three children. Sabrina was unaware that Charlie was a drug dealer because of the lies he told about being a co-owner of a janitorial business, in partnership, with Mr. Morris. When they got married, Charlie was adamant about handling all of the family finances. He paid bills promptly, gave Sabrina and the kid's allowances, and took them out to movies, dinners and vacations. They lived a good life while Sabrina managed the home and her career.

One night, all hell broke loose! Charlie was supposed to be on one of his routine late-night janitorial jobs, when in reality he was doing his usual thing—selling drugs. Two of his pushers double-crossed him and skimmed money off the top. As soon as Charlie counted the money and discovered that his money was short, he shot the two men. Before he could call for help to dispose of the bodies, the FBI nabbed him because the two men were undercover cops who had been reporting all of Charlie's activities. Charlie was sentenced to death by lethal injection.

Poor Sabrina! In her despair, she started drinking heavily and became increasingly depressed. Grandma Johnson took her to the doctor who prescribed Xanax. The Xanax was a catalyst to drug dependence, and she started taking Klonopin and OxyContin. Soon she became a drug addict selling everything that she could get her hands on, including her body, to support her habit. Sabrina was hooked and couldn't get that "monkey off her back"; she reached a point of no return and lost everything—her job, her home and her three kids. When Child Protective Services stepped in, the court awarded their custody to Grandma Johnson.

Charlie and Sabrina are in the criminal justice system, and they are a part of the big picture of black men and women in prison for selling drugs, neglecting, abusing, and losing their children. They are also there for numerous other crimes associated with drugs.

It was a happy day for Grandma Johnson when she received custody of her three grandchildren: **KEITH, JEANNIE** and **SANDRA**. She wanted to keep them together in a stable environment, give them a sense of security, and help them learn and grow. Grandma Johnson knew that there would be challenges and that she would have to make some major adjustments; however, she wanted to make a positive impact on their lives. She held back the distress of handling the additional responsibilities of caring for the children and her double grief: Sabrina's drug addiction and loss of her children as well as Charlie's imprisonment. During a trying and difficult time in her life, her golden years, Grandma Johnson was able to do what she does best, she relied on spiritual guidance and love.

One night, Grandma Johnson's youngest granddaughter, Jeannie, asked her, "Grandma why do we have to stay here with you, and how long do we have to stay here?" The other children also wanted to know. But Grandma's only response was: "My dear children, it's a long and complicated story. Let's wait until our Sunday visit with Uncle John and Aunt Mildred. They will explain the story and some other things, OK?" The children were therefore content because they loved their Sunday visits with Uncle John and Aunt Mildred.

Grandma Johnson could not explain the story of why and how the children came to live with her because she is suffering from sickle cell anemia. Sickle cell anemia is an inherited form of anemia, a condition in which there aren't enough healthy red blood cells to carry adequate oxygen to the body's tissues. Grandma Johnson was frequently fatigued and weak. She also has pulmonary hypertension and cannot remember a lot of details. She wanted her grandchildren to know the "story behind the story." Sickle cell was not the only reason that Grandma could not tell the story in the detail that she wanted to tell. She also lacks the knowledge and ability to do so because she only went to the seventh grade. In the meantime, it pleased Grandma that the grandchildren were excited about their Sunday visit with Uncle John and Aunt Mildred.

Sunday for the Johnsons is all about worship, family and fellowship. Aunt Mildred usually begins preparing for Sunday's dinner on Saturday night, rinsing the rice and destemming the collard greens. Then, she presses hers and Uncle John's outfits until they are wrinkle free. She pays careful attention to every seam and fold of her dress, especially the midnight blue A-line that she loves so much. She pairs it with a silk scarf that she purchased from a local craftswoman in Cairo, Egypt (it was one of several she bought). And she always tops off her "Sunday best" outfit with a unique hat from Sister Loretta's boutique. Her hats are elegant and elaborate, and the one that matches her blue outfit is shiny with a huge tilted brim and quaint bow around the top. Uncle John's outfits are equally sharp— he owns the finest wool suits in town. It is important for them to look their best every time they enter the house of God. By the time Aunt Mildred finishes preparing for Sunday, she is always good and tired.

Sundays come with warm embraces from Aunt Mildred and Uncle John. After a good breakfast, they arrive at church a few minutes early to greet their friends and give their respects to the Mother of the church. They enjoy lively worship and sermons from their beloved Bishop and they participate in the church services often. Uncle John volunteers as an usher, and Aunt Mildred occasionally teaches a Sunday school class. They love their church family dearly and often invite other families to eat at their home after church service.

The grandchildren love Uncle John and Aunt Mildred and enjoy visiting their home. They grew up hearing about them; Grandma Johnson holds them in high esteem, and they were Sabrina's role models.

UNCLE JOHN is Grandma Johnson's sister's son. He was raised in a mostly segregated southern city in a family that valued faith, hard work and determination. His father expected him to always remember who he was and what he was capable of as a black man. He had grandparents who valued religion and enterprise, as well as, loving uncles and aunts. He was the eldest of his siblings and was a model for them. From a young age, Uncle John learned to be self-sufficient. He started working in his grandad's neighborhood confectionary while in elementary school and eventually took a job as a paper boy. It was then that he experienced racism and discrimination more pervasively when he won a contest to increase customers on his paper route. He won for two years, receiving round trips to Miami Beach, FL, but he was not permitted to stay at the two beautiful, relatively new hotels on the beach. He had to stay at a hotel for Negroes in Miami, while the white paper boys stayed in Miami Beach as the contest advertised.

Uncle John excelled in his segregated high school, received an academic scholarship, and attended this old, elite historically black college (HBCU). There, he made international friends for the first time, including Africans and West Indians and those he played with on his college's soccer team. After a year in college, circumstances led him to join the United States Air Force (USAF) where he served nearly four years. He was stationed for several months stateside and then spent three years in Europe. He was honorably discharged and began studying chemistry at a southern HBCU. A professor encouraged him to study psychology, which he did, and he eventually earned his Bachelor's degree. Later he earned his Master's and Ph.D. degrees in psychology from a major midwestern university along with prestigious fellowships, an internship and an externship, both at a state mental health facility in an urban center.

Aunt Mildred and Uncle John got married after they graduated from college. He worked for several years at an HBCU and for a few more at a non-HBCU helping to establish doctoral programs in psychology at both. He got tired of the power politics on the predominantly white campus and concluded that his time could be better spent providing mental health services for underserved communities in the mid-Atlantic region. He established three clinics that were very productive and provided quality mental health services. Uncle John took great pride in serving his community. His work, expertise and dedication eventually earned him important roles in psychological organizations, which he takes very seriously.

AUNT MILDRED is Uncle John's wife. She comes from a large family that was tight-knit and full of typical family drama. She loved to read and study, and from a young age she dreamed of traveling and exploring the world. Aunt Mildred had an incredibly close bond with her mother who influenced a huge part of her early adult life. Of her siblings, Aunt Mildred was the studious one, the one who her mother predicted would "get out and be completely independent." She was the first of 12 children to earn a college degree.

After earning her bachelor's degree, Aunt Mildred studied Urban Administration at a major southern university. She excelled brilliantly and eventually earned her doctorate in Public Administration from that university. She served as an administrator and taught at three HBCU's. She also launched a lucrative consulting business. Aunt Mildred excelled in the consulting industry and soon gained contracts in private industry and with government agencies. She won numerous awards and now travels (just like her mother said she would) to places like London, Paris, Dubai; Guinea, West Africa; South Africa and Guantanamo Bay, Cuba. She even went back to school to earn a Master's of Divinity. Aunt Mildred is well-rounded and holds her own, and with Uncle John by her side, they are the ultimate power couple.

Uncle John and Aunt Mildred live in a Victorian mansion in the suburbs of New Jersey. It is a wealthy and predominantly African-American neighborhood that attracts mayors, senators, lawyers and the like. The area is quiet and suburban like, even though it is not far from the bustle of downtown. Aunt Mildred and Uncle John like it because the neighbors always look out for each other. Furthermore, their home is within a short commute to the college campus where he works.

Their home is extravagant and inviting. The hardwood floors are original, and Aunt Mildred decorated beautifully with pieces that she and Uncle John had collected throughout their travels. The house contained spacious extra bedrooms; one is used as a home office, another as a study room, and the third as a large guest room. The rooms downstairs are great for entertaining, something that the couple does often. They especially love Sunday visits with Grandma Johnson and the three kids.

First Sunday Visit to Uncle John and Aunt Mildred's Home

Uncle John and Aunt Mildred welcomed Grandma Johnson and the kids.

"Jeannie you are growing like a weed—and so pretty. You, too, Sandra," Aunt Mildred said, grabbing Keith and hugging him.

Uncle John asked, "What's going on with you, my man? You're sharp." Keith smiled and returned Uncle John's hug.

Aunt Mildred said, "Let's go on to the dining room because I know you're hungry."

Grandma Johnson said, "Sure, you're right! Pastor Stokes was in high spirit today. He waxed and walked the word, and the choir sang two extra songs. It was a long service!"

"Yes, too long," chuckled Keith and the other children. So off they went to the dining room.

The dining room is large and casual. The table can seat ten comfortably. The dining chairs are padded and a chandelier hangs overhead. The table allows for both warm foods and wet glasses to be placed on it without damage. The chairs can also be wiped off. It is interesting to note that Uncle John and Aunt Mildred always maintain a place setting (plate with silver ware, water glass and napkin) and a beautiful artificial red rose in front of it. The seat is never occupied because it is in honor of a loved one that has gone to glory. It is an African tradition which they honor. The room has plenty of natural light and sconces on the back wall for them to use when additional lighting is needed. The only accessories they have are a large mirror, floor-to-ceiling curtains and items on the window sill.

Grandma Johnson, the children, Aunt Mildred and Uncle John joined hands as Uncle John prayed and blessed the food. He always started with Psalm 100 (KJV):

> *Make a joyful noise unto the Lord, all ye lands. Serve the Lord with gladness: come before his presence with singing. Know ye that the LORD he is God: it is he that hath made us, and not we ourselves; we are his people, and the sheep of his pasture. Enter into his gates with thanksgiving, and into his courts with praise: be thankful unto him, and bless his name. For the Lord is good; his mercy is everlasting; and his truth endureth to all generations.*

Then he prayed: "Be present at our table, Lord. We give you the thanks for this food, food in a world where many walk in hunger, for drink when others are thirsty, for our family, gathered here, and for our love and for your love. We thank thee for our daily bread. Amen."

Their Sunday dinner was excellent: traditional soul food (chicken, macaroni, and collards) and a special African side dish which Aunt Mildred cooked every Sunday. Her African friends gave her recipes and taught her how to prepare them when she visited their country. This Sunday she prepared Jollof rice and briefly told the children about it. Jollof rice is a West African dish consumed throughout Senegal, Gambia, Nigeria, Sierra Leone, Liberia, Togo, Cameroon,

Mali and Ghana. Ingredients in Jollof rice include: rice, tomatoes, tomato paste, onions, salt and such spices as nutmeg, ginger, pepper and cumin. Aunt Mildred also added fish (because they were having fried chicken): other times she may use beef. She always added vegetables even though she fixed collards. In addition to the Jollof rice, she served fried plantains. The children and Grandma Johnson were always full of questions, and Aunt Mildred and Uncle John loved answering them.

After dinner it was "show time" for Uncle John!

Uncle John's History of Africa

They all adjourned to the family room which was Uncle John's pride and joy. The family room was a huge, informal and multi-purposed room; however, it was mainly where family, friends and guests gathered to chat, listen to music, play games and engage in other activities. Uncle John and Aunt Mildred had the family room decorated primarily in African motif with eclectic memorabilia from their international travels. The family room had a fully stocked entertainment center with a 100 inch flat screen TV, gaming devices and a large, beautiful map of Africa which was most captivating. Uncle John invited them to join him to look at the map, and he began to explain to the children why Grandma Johnson told them that explaining why they were living with her instead of their parents was a very long and complicated story. Uncle John said that both he and Grandma Johnson wanted them to understand some African history and some of the problems that their parents and other

African Americans often encounter.

He started by asking them: "Where were the first humans born?"

As they looked at each other puzzled, one of them simply said, "I don't know."

Upon hearing that, Uncle John said, "My dear children, let me teach you something about our history."

He explained that the human race was born in Africa. The skeletons, skulls, bones and other finds throughout east and south-central Africa proved that people of a Negroid type, likely originated in south-central Africa (although that is up for debate), were not only the first humans, but also influential contributors to social, economic and cultural development throughout the ancient world. A definitive study led by Andrea Manica and her team at the University of Cambridge, England in 2007 supported this by studying the skulls and DNA of ancient human remains from around the world. They found that the further away from Africa the remains were, the less diverse their genes were, mirrored by reduced physical variation. In the most remote regions relative to Africa, Australia and South America, the team found the lowest variation of features. There were no other populations contributing to the gene pool at that time. Simply put, there are no others in our family tree.[1]

"Let's fast forward a few thousand years. Now, the word 'civilized' is not a word that has been used to describe ancient Africans;

[1] Owen, J. (2007, July 18). National Geographic News. Retrieved from National Geographic: http://news.nationalgeographic.com/news/2007/07/070718- african-origin.html

however, Africa birthed the world's first great civilization known to man: Egypt. Egypt is a Greek word meaning 'Black.' Formed around 3100 BC through a union of organized states in the Nile Delta, Egypt was culturally and scientifically sophisticated. Agriculture, construction, mathematics, astronomy and language were developed and mastered by its people, and they were ruled by kings called Pharaohs within highly structured societies.[2] Egyptian civilization thrived for nearly 3,000 years and was eventually overrun by the Nubians who were early inhabitants of the Central Nile Valley.

"Many African empires throughout the continent flourished prior to the European slave trade. They include Carthage, the sixth century sea-trading city-state responsible for creating the Phoenician alphabet; Aksum, an indigenous state in the heart of Ethiopia which founded the Ethiopian Orthodox Church and was home to the legendary Queen of Sheba; and Mali, a hugely wealthy, trade-based empire which was rich in natural resources and traded with North Africa and the Middle East. On the East Coast, Swahili sultans ruled organized and rich city-states in modern-day Tanzania, Kenya and Mozambique.

"During this time African kings, queens and warriors abounded, yet we do not hear about many of them today. They include: Imhotep, one of ancient Egypt's greatest and most intelligent pharaohs; Shaka Zulu, King of Zulu, South Africa from 1818-1828, who was a famed warrior and fighter; and most notably, Mansa Mussa, King of Mali from 1306-1332 who was a great leader and economist.[3] Another

---

[2] History. (n.d.). Retrieved from Lonely Planet: http://www.lonelyplanet.com/africa/history
[3] Chigozie, E. (n.d.). 5 Most Powerful African Kings From History. Retrieved from Answers Africa: http://answersafrica.com/african-kings.html

great leader of the ancient African world was also the Empress of Ethiopia. This formidable black Queen Candace was famous as a military tactician and field commander.[4]

"In addition to great African Kings, some of the earliest contributions of Africans included the following:

- Stone Age Negroes laid the foundation for much of the civilization of the Nile Valley and manufactured pottery before pottery was made in the world's earliest known city.
- African mariners explored the New World before Columbus.
- They made realistic portraitures of Negro Africans in clay, gold and stone unearthed in pre-Columbian strata in Central and South America.
- Peoples of a Negro type were painting men and women with a beautiful and sensitive realism before 3000 B.C. and were, perhaps, the originators of naturalistic human portraiture.
- Blacks were among the first to use tools, paint pictures and worship gods.
- Black people marched in the front ranks of the emerging human procession. They founded empire states, they extended the boundaries of the possible. They made some of the critical discoveries and contributions that led to the modern world.

---

[4] Savvy Sista. (2007). African Queens: Candace- Empress of Ethiopia (332 B.C.). Retrieved from The Savvy Sista: http://www.thesavvysista.com/2007/10/african-queens-candace-empress-of.html

- Blacks were known and honored throughout the ancient world."[5]

Although Uncle John wanted the children, as well as Grandma Johnson, to know some things about African history, he did not want to turn them off or overload them with too much information.

He was delighted when Keith, the 13-year-old, said, "Uncle John, I heard that Africa was a rich continent and white folks have always been stealing their stuff and making slaves out of Africans. Can you please tell us something about that?"

Uncle John was delighted to share some more of his wisdom. He started with some basics and explained that Africa was one of the earth's seven continents or major divisions of land. Asia is the largest, he noted, and Africa is the second largest (followed by North America, South America, Antarctica, Europe and Australia). Because of Africa's known natural resources and mineral wealth, it is among the world's richest continents. It contains a very large share of the world's mineral resources such as diamonds, salt, gold, silver, platinum, natural gas, petroleum, copper, and cocoa beans. It also has wood and tropical fruits.

"You see," Uncle John said, "the natural resources of Africa could easily be converted into some big money-making businesses. So, the Atlantic slave trade, Arab slave trade and Maafa developed. Dr. Orisode Awodolu, in a personal note, said that Europeans used 'The Seasoning Process' to enslave Africans and to keep them subservient."

---

5 Bennett, L. (1984). Before the Mayflower. Penguin Books.

Grandma Johnson and the children were excited and interested in African history. Uncle John told them that he would tell them more next Sunday. He had seen Grandma Johnson occasionally nodding off and the six-year-old, Jeannie, continued her frowning and fidgeting.

Everyone was surprised when Sandra, the eleven-year-old, asked, "Uncle John, will you and Aunt Mildred please tell us more about Maafa? We've never heard of that word before."

Aunt Mildred said, "We sure will. Grandma, since we were so stuffed after dinner, would you like your dessert in a doggie bag?"

"Girl, you know that's right!" she responded, with a great big grin as the kids started smiling and clapping.

Aunt Mildred packed up the dessert, six big slices of her award-winning lemon pound cake, and they headed for the front door.

Uncle John had them all join hands for a departing prayer which he always did. This evening it was a paraphrase of Psalm 91:2-4:

"Thank You for our time together and for how You bless us. Thank You, Lord, for You alone are our refuge, our place of safety. You are our God and we trust You for You will rescue us from every trap and protect us. You will cover us with Your feathers and shelter us with Your wings. Your faithful promises are armour and protection in all that we do and wherever we go. Now bless my family members with traveling grace and mercy until we meet again. Amen."

They hugged, kissed, and headed to the car for Aunt Mildred to drive them home.

John said to Mildred, "Sweetheart, do you think that it will be a good idea to invite Grandma and the children to some of the lectures at the university and to your Family and Community Empowerment Forums at city hall? They will probably get a lot of insight from the PowerPoint graphics and technology."

"Honey, that's a great idea," Mildred replied.

John added, "I'll focus on Keith's and Sandra's questions next Sunday, then I'll give Grandma the schedule for my lecture and forums. Now, hurry back and get ready for some grown folk's business!"

Three Blind Mice

Uncle John and Aunt Mildred had their usual week. Uncle John taught his part-time class at the university and Aunt Mildred worked on some community development projects. It was a good week for Grandma Johnson and the kids too. She was delighted when they asked her to pick up some African history books, which she did, and the kids started to read them.

The children couldn't wait to visit Uncle John and Aunt Mildred.

"I wonder what we are going to have for dinner today," Sandra said.

"Yea, me too," grinned Keith.

The Baby Girl said, "You know it's going to include something African because that's Aunt Mildred's thing!"

Grandma Johnson simply said, "Just remember your manners and behave."

Uncle John started the afternoon with prayer. Then he asked about the church service and Pastor Stokes' sermon. He was surprised when Keith told him that the sermon was entitled "How to Win" (from Corinthians 9:19-27) and that Pastor Stokes left them with three things to remember: commitment, awareness and discipline. Grandma Johnson was proud to know that Keith had paid attention to the pastor's takeaways or the three points that he always tried to leave with the congregation.

Aunt Mildred served an excellent Egyptian meal called Koshari. It was a nourishing vegetarian dish of rice, lentils, macaroni, garlic and chickpeas combined with tomato sauce and topped off with fried onions. She also served fish. After dinner, they hurried to the family room. They were anxious to hear Uncle John tell them more about Africa.

"Uncle John," Keith started, "You said that you were gonna tell us about the Maafa today."

"I sure did," said Uncle John, "and I want to share something that I thought about after your visit last week." He stood up from his chair, walked towards the fireplace, and, as he did, began to sing a popular nursery rhyme:

Three blind mice. Three blind mice. See how they run. See how they run. They all ran after the farmer's wife, Who cut off their tails with a carving knife, Did you ever see such a sight in your life, As three blind mice?"

The children, surprised, began to laugh. "We know that song! What does that have to do with anything?"

Uncle John responded, "Maafa is a Kiswahili word meaning disaster, terrible occurrence, or great tragedy used to refer to the African Holocaust. Although the word is not even referenced in the English dictionary, Maafa is a historic and ongoing crime that affects Africans and African Americans to this day. When you asked me about that word last week, it made me think about that nursery rhyme, because it is a great representation of how Maafa has and continues to affect our world today.

"The woman in the rhyme is Maafa in its truest form. She represents imperialism, colonialism, slavery and racism. She is weaponized, in control, and in pursuit of a determined goal. The blind mice wander around without purpose, without power and without direction, and today they represent African Americans who are underpowered and scarred from Maafa's effects. The three blind conditions which affect the three mice are mental illness, miseducation and poverty. They are most notable among each mouse's ailments and are separate tragedies which plague and hinder the black community.

"To understand the development of mental illness, miseducation and poverty in the African American community today, we must consider this picture as a whole. Many want to observe, analyze and solve these problems in a vacuum, as if African Americans are the sole source of the problem.

"But, when we zoom out of the picture, we can see the woman (Maafa) and her weapon (slavery and racism). We begin to understand that the problem is much larger and much more complex than we imagined. It has a lot less to do with the 'natural' state of blacks and a lot more to do with the natural history of Europeans and white Americans. If the woman is Maafa, then the problems developed long ago. The blindness actually began in Africa.

"So, in order to fully answer your question about Maafa, we must walk together through African American history, starting in Africa. We must understand the woman's tactics and devices and how they've affected the three mice from slavery until now. We will end, as you will see, at the current state of black America, where mental illness, miseducation and poverty (the blindness) abound. The statistics here are staggering and alarming, and I will share them with you, along with some other pertinent information.

"If we were to continue reading John W. Ivimey's complete children's version of the story, we would find that the three blind mice eventually use a tonic to grow new tails and regain their eyesight. My hope is that we will eventually get to that part of the story, and I have some ideas about how we can. After years of observation and collaboration with other thinkers and doers, I've found that there are many avenues through which the 'tonic' can be administered, including socially, economically, spiritually, and culturally. And, it will require a 'cradle to grave' commitment. But I think it is possible, and I've dedicated my life's work to contributing to this solution."

Uncle John's Plan

At this point, the children's mouths were on the floor in amazement. Uncle John noticed their expression and realized that he may have overwhelmed them.

"Keith, I'm afraid the answer to your question is a bit more than you bargained for, but you are in for some illumination," Uncle John remarked. "Here's what I'd like to do—if you decide to come along for the ride. First, I want you all to join me at the college for a Guest Lecture Series with Dr. Alease Cunningham. She is a psychiatrist and she will discuss the development of the first blindness that I spoke about tonight, **mental illness**. I suspect that she will draw a connection between the trauma and horrors experienced by slaves upon their capture in Africa and during the Middle Passage and the intergenerational anxiety that it has produced. She will also address common disorders experienced by African Americans including Posttraumatic Slave Syndrome (PTSS), depression, and substance abuse.

"Next, I will invite you to my lecture at the University to discuss the second blindness, **miseducation**. We will learn about the origin of miseducation in the African American community and relearn some truths that have been passed over in your schooling. This will lead to a retrospective commentary relating to the miseducation of Africa, the miseducation of the Negro, and the miseducation of

African Americans today.

"We will attend a university-wide lecture on **poverty** given by Dr. Clarence Scott from the President's Committee on Economic Development. Remember, poverty is the third blindness among the three mice. The speaker will highlight African Americans' first exposure to poverty following the Emancipation Proclamation all the way through Reconstruction, the Great Depression and the World Wars. Then, we will hear contributing factors to current poverty rates and catch a glimpse of what it means to be a poor black person in America, economically and socially.

"Throughout the lecture series, you will hear things that make you think about your parents and your family, and it is my hope that you will begin to understand some of the many factors that are involved in our family dynamic. You will learn a great deal about yourself, your parents and your community by the time we finish.

"Finally, I will have you join Aunt Mildred and me at a Family Empowerment and Community Development Summit with renowned scholars, authors and practitioners who will present some 'cradle to grave' prescriptions, recommended solutions and remedies for the three blind mice, and their contagious maladies. We will combine all of these solutions and form the 'tonic' that we hope will ultimately address and cure some of the problems we're facing today. The question now is, are you up for the journey?"

"YES!" the kids shouted.

"Ok, good! Hold on tight," Uncle John cautioned.

PART II
Mental Illness

Mental Illness

The week of waiting for the first lecture series was filled with great expectation, and the day finally came. The children waited anxiously for Uncle John and Aunt Mildred to come by and take them to the college. When they arrived, the Martin Luther King, Jr. Auditorium was packed; however, they were able to sit up front with Uncle John. The guest speaker was Dr. Alease Cunningham, a prominent psychiatrist and consultant from a government health and human service agency.

"Good afternoon. Welcome to our first Guest Lecture Series," said the host. "Our guest speaker, Dr. Alease Cunningham, wants to introduce herself. So please put your hands together and show her some love."

The students gave a thunderous standing ovation as Dr. Cunningham approached the podium. She was strikingly beautiful, clad in a vivid, bright color, a Ghanaian Kabu and slit outfit with a matching gele (head tie).

She warmly greeted the audience: "Good afternoon, thank you for inviting me. I am honored."

Then she pointed to a picture that was being projected on the screen beside the podium. It was a picture of four black people in handcuffs, kicking and fighting as two white men in uniforms pulled and pushed them through the doors of a southern state hospital—an asylum. An old lady and little girl sat on a nearby bench watching the drama unfold. She gave the audience some brief background information.

"I was born in Yazoo City, Mississippi, which is the second poorest city in the state. I was the oldest of ten children. My father worked in a lumber mill and my mother did day's work; we were dirt poor. I am the girl in that picture, eight years old; the elderly lady, Mrs. Lucy, was my neighbor. I used to go to the general store to help her count her grocery money so that the white storekeeper would not cheat her. Many white folks back then were famous for cheating Blacks, and some still do it today because they continue to think of us as dumb, liberated slaves. My neighbor also took me other places sometimes when she had to ride the bus a long way. But back to the picture. The two white men hit the people over their backs and heads, called them 'niggers' and other names.

"I still remember hearing one man continue to say, 'I am not crazy. Please don't take me in there and leave me!' I asked Mrs. Lucy what was going on and what 'crazy' meant. She told me that the people were being locked up because they were crazy. She explained that crazy meant mentally deranged, insane, mad and cannot be controlled. I told Mrs. Lucy that the man was yelling he was not crazy, but the men kept beating him anyway. I felt so sorry for the man and the other people because I believed him. I believed in my heart, my eight-year-old heart, that the man was not crazy.

"That very day I told Mrs. Lucy: When I grow up, I am going to do something to help people stay out of state hospitals when they are not crazy. I am going to be a doctor."

She responded, "You're talking about a psychiatrist, girl, someone who deals with peoples' minds."

Dr. Cunningham explained: "I like to show that picture because it gave me a dream and a goal for my life. I can't begin to tell you how it broke my heart to see people being beaten and called names. The words, 'I'm not crazy' were unforgettable and inspired me to be a psychiatrist. In undergraduate school, I majored in biology. Thereafter, I studied for and passed the Medical College Admission Test (MCAT) for medical school. After receiving my Doctor of Medicine (M.D.) at Harvard and securing my physician license, I completed a four-year psychiatric residency, board certification, post-residency fellowship training and began my private practice. I've been working in the mental health field for over 20 years. It is my commitment and passion. So let me share some salient points with you. By the way, I'd like to thank those of you who emailed the pre-lecture list of items for discussion. I will sandwich those in my lecture."

Understanding the Origin and Development of Mental Illness

"Although we are an advanced society, there is still so much for us to learn about the brain and about mental health. We have even more work to do in understanding how culture and history, including intergenerational traumatic events, affects one's mental state. Unfortunately, that means that some of the mental disorders that many of our people face go unnoticed, unacknowledged, and completely misunderstood. And, as I mentioned earlier in my story, the label 'mental illness' has also been abused to manipulate and restrict certain groups. It's my hope that as we come to fully understand this topic, that we can become more responsible in acknowledging, diagnosing and properly treating those with mental disorders, especially those within the African American community.

"Let's start with a definition and some facts: mental illness refers to a wide range of mental health conditions—including disorders that affect your mood, thinking or behavior.[6]

"According to the US Census Bureau (2013), there are 45 million people who identify as African Americans.[7] Research and statistics about their mental health indicate that there is an array of multifarious problems that need to be addressed from a historical perspective. Intergenerational and systemic adversities caused by slavery and its aftermath, including exclusion from health, education, social and financial resources, among other problems, have long combined to produce some devastating results. Let's look at one in detail, slavery.

"Trauma is a word that comes to mind when I think about the harsh and unimaginable experiences that Africans faced when

---

[6] Staff, M. C. (2015, October 15). Definition. Retrieved from Mayo Clinic: http://www.mayoclinic.org/diseases-conditions/mental- illness/basics/definition/con-20033813

[7] United States Census Bureau. (2013). American Fact Finder. Retrieved from United States Census Bureau: https://factfinder.census.gov/faces/tableservices/jsf/pages/productview.xhtml?src=bkmk

encountering traders and colonialists in their homelands. Slave narratives are essential to our understanding of the conditions and realities that slaves were exposed to, and we have access to several that were written from the perspectives of both traders and slaves. Interestingly, but not surprisingly, the accounts of slave traders justified the trade by pointing out the 'deplorable' and harsh conditions faced by Africans upon their capture and made it seem as though the traders were doing them favors by 'rescuing' them from their homelands.

"On the other hand, we have accounts like that from Venture Smith, a slave who was kidnapped and sold at six, brought to Connecticut, and purchased his freedom at 31. Venture's account, written in 1798, is harrowing and clearly demonstrates one of the many traumas experienced by Africans before they even landed in America—separation from family and torture:[8]

> They then came to us in the reeds, and the very first salute I had from them was a violent blow on the back part of the head with the fore part of a gun, and at the same time a grasp round the neck. I then had a rope put about my neck, as had all the women in the thicket with me, and were immediately led to my father, who was likewise pinioned and haltered for leading. In this condition we were all led to the camp. The women and myself being pretty submissive, had tolerable treatment from the enemy, while my father was closely interrogated respecting his money which they knew he must have. But as he gave them no account of it, he was instantly cut and pounded on his body with great inhumanity, that he might be induced by the

---

[8] Smith, V. (n.d.). Excerpts from Slave Narratives. Retrieved from UNESCO ASPnet TST: http://www.vgskole.net/prosjekt/slavrute/4.htm

torture he suffered to make the discovery. All this availed not in the least to make him give up his money, but he despised all the tortures which they inflicted, until the continued exercise and increase of torment, obliged him to sink and expire. He thus died without informing his enemies where his money lay. I saw him while he was thus tortured to death. The shocking scene is to this day fresh in my mind, and I have often been overcome while thinking on it....

"There are thousands and likely millions of similar, undocumented stories like this. Venture's trauma did not end in this moment where he witnessed his father's death and was separated from his family, it was only beginning. We know, since he became free at 31, that he experienced 25 years of slavery, which was more trauma, as well as the subsequent hardships of being a free man in an antebellum society until his death. Imagine all of that trauma being experienced in one man's lifetime. Now, think about that same trauma being felt by multiple generations of millions of people.

"We are, of course, more familiar with the dehumanizing practices of slavery in America. Extreme physical traumas like branding and amputations were the first forms of torture employed by slave owners to control slaves.[9] Later, beatings, rape, humiliation and overwork were popular and widely used to tame and control slaves. Psychological trauma was inevitable, inflicted by violence, forced obedience and forced submission. Slaves were not allowed to exhibit core emotions like fear, anger or joy, without punishment. The greatest threat to the plantation was a free-thinking, intelligent, male

---

[9] Painter, N. I. (2006, February 14). Slavery: A Dehumanizing Institution. Retrieved from OUPblog: http://blog.oup.com/2006/02/slavery_a_dehum/

slave. So, many efforts were employed as preventative tools to keep him from developing and to keep the economic engine moving.

"We, as educators and students, must seek to know and understand the history of this trauma in order to understand how it persists today. It is difficult to read about; it makes us uncomfortable and fills us with emotions, feelings and thoughts that are hard to process. I struggle even to share more slave accounts and narratives with you today, and I won't. But we cannot ignore the truth, and we cannot continue to deny the effects that this trauma has and is having on an entire race of people today. The U.S. Department of Health and Human Service, Office of Minority Statistics reveals the following:

- Adult blacks are 20 percent more likely to report serious psychological distress than adult whites.
- Adult blacks living below poverty are two to three times more likely to report serious psychological distress than those living above poverty.
- Adult blacks are more likely to have feelings of sadness, hopelessness, and worthlessness than are adult whites.
- And while blacks are less likely than whites to die from suicide as teenagers, black teenagers are more likely to attempt suicide than are white teenagers (8.2 percent v. 6.3 percent). [10]

[10] Mental Health and African Americans. (n.d.). Retrieved from U.S. Department of Health and Human Services Office of Minority Health: http://minorityhealth.hhs.gov/omh/browse.aspx?lvl=4&lvlID=24

"Is it possible that the traumas experienced by slaves like Venture and millions of others contribute to these statistics? Many believe not, but I unashamedly say, 'Yes, they do. Completely.' There are so many current problems and concerns that warrant our attention and understanding; however, I want to briefly give an overview of the ways in which trauma has affected 'the whole man.' This will be a discussion on a controversial topic and condition known as Posttraumatic Slave Syndrome (PTSS). Then, I will follow with a more in-depth look at the theories of Dr. Frances Cress Welsing as well as the phenomenon known as 'black rage.'

"Next, I will cover three major mental illnesses which disproportionately affect the African American community today: schizophrenia, bipolar disorder and depression. I call them 'The Big Three.' Finally, I will end with some predictions regarding mental health in the black community.

Posttraumatic Slave Syndrome

"Posttraumatic Slave Syndrome is a theory which explains some key patterns of behavior among African Americans today which are a direct result of the residual impacts trauma of slavery. These key patterns are consequential, multigenerational conditions which have emerged and developed from systemic, indoctrinated, institutionalized, and internalized oppression and manifest in some disturbing and destructive ways.

"I am finding that there is a lack of effective mental health treatments for African Americans, and this is largely because they are misunderstood and misplaced within the historical and cultural spectra of mental health. Simply put, traditional mental health systems were not designed to consider the traumatic effects of slavery on African Americans. They tend to be Eurocentric and often ignore much of the triggers that African Americans are facing, even today. I find the PTSS theory so enlightening and necessary because it forces us to really consider the reality of our past and acknowledge the real effect it has on our lives.

"When we carefully examine some of the key patterns of behavior of PTSS identified by Reid, Mims and Higginbottom in *Posttraumatic Slavery Disorder*, so much of the current mental state of black America begins to make sense. The key patterns include: low self-esteem, anger and violence, racist socialization, avoidance, emotional numbing, and poor diet and health.[11] Let's look at the chart which follows and talk about these patterns individually.

---

[11] Reid, Mims and Higginbottom's *Posttraumatic Slavery Disorder* and Joy DeGruy's *Posttraumatic Slave Syndrome*

Key Patterns of Posttraumatic Slave Syndrome

Key Pattern	Current Manifestation	Slavery Manifestation
Anger and Violence	-Violence against self, property and others (esp. within race). - High levels of suspicion and mistrust; always on the lookout for who's out to get who.	-Extreme acts of violence, torture, and anger were directed towards slaves, often unexpectedly. -Removal of many means of self-defense.
Internalized Racism	-Learned helplessness. -Light-skinned vs. dark-skinned comparisons. -Antipathy and aversion.	-Some slaves worked slowly and inefficiently as a strategic means to slow production. -Light-skinned slaves-often the result of slavemaster's affairs with black women- were often treated better and allowed to work as house servants. -Many slaves who were left in charge in the slave master's absence were abusive, assuming their master's identity and traits.
Avoidance	-Most African Americans don't want to talk or hear about slavery at all because it causes anger and feelings of hopelessness. -There is a disinterest in African history and genealogy among African Americans; some don't want to be associated with Africa.	-Slaves were tortured and killed for speaking their native languages or sharing their histories. -Most slaves were not allowed to learn how to read or write and faced severe punishments for attempting to do so.

Emotional Numbing	-High divorce rates and high rates of single parenthood. -Black males are often disconnected from their children. -Substance abuse.	-Slaves were forced to watch their loved ones being brutalized, murdered or sold. -Slave masters allowed marriages and relationships for the sake of breeding and often tore families apart. -Black men were not allowed to maintain control of their families; children were to be raised by their mothers to be submissive to authority.
Poor Diet and Health	-Poor eating habits (prevalence of foods that are high in fat, carbohydrates, sugar, and sodium- what we call "soul-food"). -High rates of diabetes, high blood pressure, high cholesterol.	-Slaves were given 'scraps' to eat, which included the unused parts of the animals that slave masters didn't want (i.e., pig's feet, chitterlings, turkey necks, etc.). -Slaves often cooked with a lot of butter and seasonings to make their food edible.

"When we study the writings of those like Willie Lynch, who dedicated his efforts to taming and controlling slaves for the highest economic impact, one thing becomes very clear: these sociological traumas were meant to be transferred from generation to generation. At its peak, slavery was imagined to be carried out for centuries, and people like Lynch devised complex and sophisticated plans to make sure that would happen. And the funny thing is that it has happened, and now no one wants to talk about it. It's one of those things that make you go, 'Hmm…'

"Now, let's consider some common symptoms of traditional Posttraumatic Stress Disorder (PTSD), which include intense fear, persistent flashbacks of the traumatic event, numbing, intrusive thoughts, aggression, nightmares and isolation. It can be argued that PTSD among African Americans may really fall under the umbrella of PTSS. This is a theory that we must seriously acknowledge in order to address some underlying problems of mental illness within our mental health systems.

"One remarkable thought leader in our time was Dr. Frances Cress Welsing, who held some interesting and provocative theories on racism and white supremacy. A graduate of Antioch College, Dr. Welsing was a practicing psychiatrist in Washington, D.C., until her death in January 2016. She is most known for her *Cress Theory of Color Confrontation* and for *The Isis Papers*.

"There were several postulates of Dr. Welsing which help us understand why her ideas were rejected by many mainstream intellectuals. First, Dr. Welsing asserted that Africa was the origin of civilization and that advancements in science, philosophy, architecture and arts were made by Africans and predate and subvert traditional Eurocentric progressions. Second, Dr. Welsing asserted that the white race was formed as a result of albinism, a genetically defective state that caused separation and isolation within the African community, possibly causing them to be forcibly expelled. In an attempt to preserve light-skinned purity, whites took a dominant and aggressive stance towards others. She further posited that whites' melanin deficiency accounts for some inherent behavioral differences between Blacks and whites.

"According to Welsing, racism and white supremacy is the system through which whites attempt to maintain dominance and preserve their race from genetic annihilation. It represents the motivation behind trauma inflicted on Blacks during slavery. At the same time, whites desire the abilities and natural traits that their black, melanin-rich ancestors possessed, and have formed a sense of self-hatred because they lack it. Their oppressive behavior is merely an overcompensation for their insecurities. Interesting concept, isn't it? Here's Dr. Welsing's full, functional definition of racism:

> *Racism and white supremacy is the local and global power system and dynamic, structured and maintained by people who classify themselves as white—whether consciously or subconsciously determined, which consists of patterns of perception, logic, symbol formation, thoughts, speech actions and emotional response, as conducted simultaneously in all areas of people activity, including economics, education, entertainment, labor, law, politics, religion, sex and war—for the ultimate purpose of white genetic survival and to prevent white genetic annihilation on planet Earth, the planet which upon the vast and overwhelming majority of people are classified as non-white (black brown red and yellow), by white-skinned people and all of the non-white people are genetically dominant in terms of skin coloration compared to the genetic recessive white-skinned people.*[12]

"A third assertion which has garnered much criticism from Welsing's opponents is that homosexuality, bisexuality and black male effeminization are tools used by white supremacists to encourage black passivity and submissiveness. Where the 'primary effeminacy' of whites is attributed to whites' psychological disgust

---

[12] Charles, M. (2013, December 22). Author Interview: Dr. Frances Cress Welsing. Retrieved from Knowshi: http://knowshi.com/author-interview-dr-frances-cress-welsing/

with their own genetic state and subconscious desire not to produce. Black 'secondary effeminacy' is imposed on black men as a weapon to destroy black families. Although her concepts are radical in thought, they provide some insight that is worth exploring and expanding the PTSS theory quite a bit.

Black Rage

"There is one pattern on the PTSS chart that I'd like for us to examine closely, and that is 'anger and violence.' Following a turbulent and racially tense decade, including the assassination of Dr. Martin Luther King, Jr., two black psychiatrists, William Greer and Price Cobbs, penned a critical examination of African Americans titled *Black Rage*. It was published in 1968 and reached an unanticipated wide audience.

"Greer and Cobbs used a series of case studies to demonstrate many of the things that we're talking about today and which support the notion that African Americans bear the burden of living in a society which has historically undermined, feared and misunderstood their plight. As a result of trying to fit in (i.e., black women changing their appearance to adhere to European standards of beauty, black men who must work to not seem threatening or angry), a deep sense of resentment developed and remains today. Suspicion and paranoia, then, are naturally occurring postures in African Americans which have proven necessary for survival.[13]

---

[13] Morgan, J. (2016). Review: Black Rage. Retrieved from Culture + Youth Studies: http://cultureandyouth.org/african-american-culture/books- african-american-culture/black-rage/

"The term 'black rage' became popular again in 1994 during the notorious mass murder trial of Colin Ferguson, a black man who shot and killed several people while aboard a train in New York. Black rage, as a psychological phenomenon, was proposed by Ferguson's lawyers as an explanation for his acts. Ferguson was found guilty on all charges. Yet the trial did reintroduce Greer and Cobb's concept and prompted national attention.

"Since then, we have not heard much about that particular term, but I believe that we are seeing evidence of it at unmistakable levels today. Consider the passionate response we've seen to police brutality and discrimination in the form of the Black Lives Matter Movement. What if we began to seriously consider PTSS and black rage the same way we consider PTSD, battered women defense, and child abuse syndrome? Is that even possible in today's world? I think about the many stereotypes and caricatures that are perpetuated in the media about African Americans, including the image of the 'angry black woman,' and the 'aggressive black thug,' and wonder when these psychological explanations will begin to carry any real weight.

"Keep in mind that my goal is to raise your awareness about mental illness and various problems that may be all around you. I want us to draw connections between the past and the present. In no way am I asserting that slavery is the sole cause of every mental condition that African Americans face, or the "Big Three" mental illnesses that I am about to cover next. They are experienced by people in all walks of life and from all backgrounds. I am saying that trauma is pervasive and can have intergenerational impacts, and we must acknowledge and properly consider historical trauma when assessing and developing treatment plans for those experiencing these conditions. We can no longer say that, 'slavery is over and done with,' and that, 'we should just get over it.' I'm saying, psychologically and physiologically, we may have some real barriers which prevent us from healing.

"Now, I've prepared some slides to help us cover as much as possible about the Big Three. They include illnesses which are statistically more likely to be experienced by African Americans, and they contribute to a number of misfortunes which plague the black community such as suicide, homelessness, and incarceration.[14] I'll ask you to pay attention to the symptoms outlined here and to imagine just how many slaves (and their children, and their children's children) experienced them in their lifetimes. Think about how these symptoms are similar to the key patterns we discussed when talking about PTSS."

"Dr. Cunningham asked the audience to jot down their comments or concerns and hold them for the question and answer session.

---

[14] African American Mental Health. (n.d.). Retrieved from National Alliance on Mental Illness: http://www.nami.org/Find-Support/Diverse- Communities/African-Americans

Mental Illnesses: The Big Three

Illness	Definition	Symptoms
1. Schizophrenia	This is a brain disease that includes delusions, confusion, agitation, social withdrawal, psychosis and strange behavior.	. Lack of emotions. . Low energy. . Lack of interest in life. . Social isolation. . Inability to make or keep friends.
2. Bipolar Disorder	This is a chronic illness that affects the brain in a way that can cause extreme and negative mood swings.	. Severe fluctuations in mood. . Sad, empty and hopeless feelings. . Trouble sleeping. . Feeling worthless or very guilty.
3. Depression (includes various types: Persistent Depressive Disorder; Seasonal Affective Disorder (SAD); Psychotic Depression; Post-Partum Depression)	This is a mood disorder that causes symptoms that affect how you feel, think or handle daily activities.	. Low or irritable moods. . Tiredness or lack of energy. . Feeling hopeless or helpless. . Trouble sleeping or sleeping too . much. . Lack of activity.

"She then continued her presentation. Traditionally, there has been a negative stigma around the discussion of mental health in the African American community. This is for many reasons. First, there is a misunderstanding and lack of information about mental illness. Many African Americans equate mental illness with weakness and are ashamed to admit that they are experiencing symptoms. Second, many others distrust the health care system because of malpractice, discrimination and misdiagnosis. Additionally, there are fewer African American mental health professionals in the field. Third, African Americans tend to turn to faith and spirituality as a source of strength in the face of adversity, but, too often, 'relying on God' turns into a denial of much needed medical care.

"My prediction is that the collective mental health and mental illness of the black community will continue to fail unless drastic efforts are made to acknowledge and address the patterns and symptoms of Posttraumatic Slave Syndrome, Posttraumatic Stress Disorder and black rage. Anger and mistrust are mounting in the face of systemic or institutional racism. It is also rising up as a result of everyday or overt racism. People are becoming fed up. African Americans are also beginning to realize that mental health is a priority, and are talking more openly about it. I believe that a lot of pressure is about to be put on policymakers and educators to make education more accessible for those who desire to train professionally to treat illnesses in the African American community. But unless some real, effective responses are seen on multiple levels, the forces which contribute to black rage will continue to build. Thank you for your time, and it is my hope that we discussed some things today that will cause you to think and to take action for your mental health and others."

Grandma Johnson was pensive as they left the campus and headed for home; however, the children were chatty and asked a lot of questions.

Sandra, the oldest granddaughter, asked Aunt Mildred a very interesting one: "Dr. Cunningham is not African, so why did she wear that outfit and wrap her head like an African?"

"Sandra, that's an excellent question, and I'm glad you asked. The way Dr. Cunningham was dressed relates to her cultural heritage."

"Her what?" asked Jeannie, the baby granddaughter.

Aunt Mildred smiled, repeated the words and explained. She said, "Cultural heritage is the transmission of practices, engagements, and habits of a particular group. Dr. Cunningham is also an Africanist; that means she specializes in and studies African culture. She is proud of her heritage and the way she was dressed today spoke volumes. A picture is worth a thousand words, you know."

"W-O-W! That's cool!" said Jeannie.

Then Keith said, "It's a shame that they don't teach us more African history in school."

"I know, son," said Uncle John. "That is why I try to teach you as much as I can and expose you to Africa through our museum trips, lectures like the one we're attending, the library and so on."
And Keith said, "We sure do appreciate it, and we like visiting and hanging out with y'all."

"Let's hurry home and eat," Aunt Mildred said. "I cooked dinner early this morning. And yes, Jeannie, it is an African dish." They all laughed as they got in Uncle John's car and headed home.

The next morning John was excited about going to class. He had some wonderful ideas and plans for his students. John's class consisted of 20 very bright, diverse students: millennials, veterans and some seeking career changes. The thing that John liked the most was their commonalities. They were studious, dedicated and had a quest for knowledge—seemingly insatiable. John could certainly use those attributes to help take them to a higher level. What did John mean by a higher level? He simply meant augmenting his existing syllabus with more eclectic content and innovative instructions as well as student engagement strategies.

Professor Johnson opened his class with a brief summary of the Mental Health Series and gave them a one-page handout of the major points covered. He asked the students if they had heard the Three Blind Mice nursery rhyme, and he told them that he used it with his nieces and nephew in a discussion of African history. He also explained how important it is for them to not be blind about mental illnesses.

He asked the class, "How many of you attended the Guest Lecturer Series and heard Dr. Alease Cunningham speak?" Half of the class raised their hands. Professor Johnson told them that her cursory overview of what she called the Big Three: schizophrenia, bipolar disorder, and depression was only the beginning to a subject that was much bigger in scope and content and one that warranted further research and discussion.

He said, "Mental illnesses are difficult to explain and understand because there are so many different forms and some symptoms are similar. People perish because of a lack of knowledge."

He asked the class, "Why is it important to understand mental illness?" They gave some of the following answers:

- "Understanding helps to demystify stigmas and stereotypes."
- "Understanding produces compassion and empathy."
- "Understanding helps to improve relationships and helps you to help others."
- "Understanding helps to overcome prejudice and discrimination."

Professor Johnson explained that mental health is essential to quality of life, healthy relationships, good choices, well-being and the ability to cope with life's ups and downs. He was pleased with the answers that students provided and the stimulating discussions which followed. Since student engagement was at an all-time high and the class chemistry was excellent, Professor Johnson decided to step things up a notch. The night before, he prayed and meditated for guidance to take his class to the next level.

While students were talking, his answer came: "Let your students do some of the work," was his divine mandate.

Professor Johnson stopped talking and divided the class into four groups. He projected the first slide of the PowerPoint that he was going to show and discuss. The slide listed four topics: 1. Anxiety, 2. Depression, 3. Alcohol Abuse, and 4. Narcotics Abuse. He assigned one topic to each group.

He said, "I want you to research your topic and prepare a

presentation which can include, but may not be limited to: a mini-research paper, annotated bibliography, essay, documented and summarized interview with a subject matter expert (e.g., a psychiatrist, social worker or renowned author), case study, prepared lecture or something of your choice. I am giving you a carte blanche to develop a quality product. Please use the rest of the class to plan, draft a preliminary outline and discuss it with me. Your final presentations are due at midterm as listed on the syllabus."

Each group brainstormed ideas for their assigned topic and shared their preliminary plan with Professor Johnson. Group I (Anxiety Disorder) would present a case study; Group II (Depression) a report; Group III (Substance Abuse: Alcohol) a problem and solution discussion; and Group IV (Substance Abuse: Narcotics) a panel discussion. Professor Johnson was delighted as he watched the students work in the groups and more so with the plans that resulted.

When he got home, he rushed inside and called Mildred.

"Mildred, honey, come downstairs so I can share my good news!" he shouted with excitement.

"What is it dear?" she asked.

John told Mildred about the assignments he gave his students and their preliminary plans. Mildred shared his joy and excitement.

As she headed for the kitchen to prepare dinner, she looked at John and said, "God is good."

He said, "The prayers of the righteous availeth much."

Mildred and John had a wonderful dinner and loving night. Their time together was always more intimate and pleasurable when everything was great in all areas of their lives. John's energy and stamina were at an all-time high, and Mildred kept up with him, like Lionel Richie says, "All night long."

"They were awakened the next morning by a cell phone call from Grandma Johnson. She wanted to give them a praise report about the children.

When John answered the phone, she said, "Good morning, John, please forgive me for calling this early, but I wanted to give you some good news before I leave for work. First of all, I have to thank you and Mildred for all that you do to help me with the children. You have no idea how much the time we spend with you and Mildred means to us. John, they got their report cards, and the three of them made the honor roll. They have adjusted to living with me, and they enjoy the times we spend together. They even like the African dishes that Mildred serves on Sunday."

John interrupted Grandma Johnson because he knew she was on a roll; he wanted to cut the conversation before she started shouting or crying.

"Granny," he said, "that is indeed a good news report. Mildred and I truly enjoy the children, and we are committed to their emotional well-being. We will always support you and help the kids in any way we can. I just want you to keep up the good job you're doing, okay

Sis? Gotta get up and get going. Love you. Say hello to the kids for Mildred and me and have a blessed day."

"Will do Bro," said Grandma. "Love you more. Take care. Bye now."

John and Mildred eased into the day: light breakfast, reading the newspaper, sharing agenda for the day and off to work for both of them.

There were three weeks until student presentations were due. Time passed slowly for John, but quickly for the students, and they were ready when the time came. John invited Mildred, Grandma Johnson, and several colleagues to the students' presentations. Since Dr. Cunningham was in town on a consultation assignment, John also invited her to attend.

The campus was very busy: the library was crowded, the computer labs were full, and some professors begin to see their missing in action students return to class to brownnose while pretending to be on top of things. Professors were accustomed to mid-term dynamics, but they were more anxious to see students' mastery of the course contents whether through exams or special projects.

Professor Johnson arrived on campus early to make sure everything was in order and ready when his class arrived. Several groups also came to class early to prepare for presentation. As the bell sounded to end the class that was in session, the students rushed into Professor Johnson's class.

"Good afternoon, my bright, stellar students. This is the day that I'm sure we've all been waiting for. It's midterm!" he said with a big grin and open arms. "Before we get started, I want to go over a few rules: give the presenters your undivided attention; do not talk while a group presentation is in progress; turn off all cell phones at this time and put them away; take notes and jot down comments; and hold your questions until the end of a presentation. You have 20 minutes max to present."

The first presentation was on anxiety from group one, and it was a case study.

> June is a 35-year-old, separated mother of three children. As a child, June was often teased for her dark complexion and made to feel as an outcast, even within her own family. June became obsessive about her looks, her hair and her outfits. June married young to a well-to-do man, and they had children early.
>
> Her husband provided for the family, but he was an alcoholic and had a bad temper. Many nights, he would fight June, and the kids would have to come in and beg him to stop. Other nights, June would wait up for her husband to come home; instead, he would hang out all night in the bar.
>
> June eventually separated from her husband, leaving her to manage the household and take care of their three children on her own. She kept the house during the day and worked throughout the night, barely making enough to support the family.
>
> One evening last month, June received a phone call from her mother-in-law that her husband had gone missing again. He is known to hang around the streets often, and it is rumored that

he is on drugs.

Over the last year, June has not been able to shake some very
negative and pessimistic thoughts. She has become restless,
tired, tense and cannot sleep at night. She often paces around
the house, mumbling things to herself and losing her train of
thought. At night, she mentally rehearses all of the worst case
scenarios involving her husband and their family. She is
concerned that he will never return and that she will be unable
to maintain their family alone.

The group leader presented evidence to suggest that June was
suffering from an anxiety disorder:

- June began experiencing excessive and persistent worry
- June's anxiety impacted her day-to-day activities
- She started showing compulsive and obsessive symptoms
- She became persistently tired and could not sleep at night

"June's symptoms are indicative of Generalized Anxiety Disorder
(GAD), a condition that about four million adult Americans suffer
from during the course of a year," the group leader explained. "For
those people, daily life becomes a constant state of dread, fear and
worry. So much so that everyday activities are hindered, like in
June's case. Many who suffer from GAD experience worries that are
unrealistic, and while June certainly does face some hard
circumstances, her ability to cope with them properly appears
hindered.

"June's plight is an all-too common one in the black community,"
she continued in closing. "Several weeks ago, at the Empowerment

Conference, we discussed some of the problems plaguing the black community, and many of them definitely seem to be present here. We even discussed among the group whether PTSS might be at play here. It likely is and has contributed to the patterns exhibited by both June, who has been obsessed with her looks and resents her dark complexion, as well as her husband, who struggles with alcohol and potential drug abuse. This case study makes us wonder, as a group, how many men and women are experiencing GAD and PTSS and don't even realize it. This is a mental health crisis which concerns us greatly, and our group has already started researching ways to address it."

The class nodded and applauded in approval. Professor Johnson was greatly pleased.

"The floor is open. Who's next?" asked Professor Johnson.

"We are," said a spokesperson for group two. "Our topic is depression, and our focus is on the journalistic questions: who, what, when, where, why, and how, plus some solutions. I will ask the question and a member of the group will provide answers. Are you ready for us?"

The class answered "Yes" in unison.

The spokesperson said, "First up is a definition of depression- the What. Depression is a common and serious mood disorder that causes ongoing sadness and loss of interest. It is also called major depressive disorder or clinical depression which affects how a person feels, thinks, and behaves. The way basic daily activities are handled can cause emotional and physical problems. According to the National Institute of Mental Health, there are many different types of depression.[15] Ten forms include:

1. **Persistent depressive disorder** (also called dysthymia) is a depressed mood that lasts for at least two years. A person diagnosed with persistent depressive disorder may have episodes of major depression along with periods of less severe symptoms, but symptoms must last for two years to be considered persistent depressive disorder.

2. **Perinatal depression** or postpartum depression is much more serious than the 'baby blues' (relatively mild depressive and anxiety symptoms that typically clear within two weeks after delivery) that many women experience after giving birth. Women with perinatal depression experience full-blown major depression during pregnancy or after delivery (postpartum depression). The feelings of extreme sadness, anxiety, and exhaustion that accompany perinatal depression may make it difficult for these new mothers to complete daily care activities for themselves and/or for their babies.

3. **Psychotic depression** occurs when a person has severe depression plus some form of psychosis, such as having disturbing, false fixed beliefs (delusions) or hearing or seeing upsetting things that others cannot hear or see (hallucinations). The psychotic symptoms typically have a depressive "theme," such as delusions of guilt, poverty, or illness. *Folie à deux*, which is related to psychotic depression, is now present in our political system.

4. **Seasonal affective disorder** is characterized by the onset of depression during the winter months, when there is less natural sunlight. This depression generally lifts during spring and

---

[15] (n.d.). Retrieved from National Institute of Mental Health: https://www.nimh.nih.gov/index.shtml

summer. Winter depression, typically accompanied by social withdrawal, increased sleep, and weight gain, predictably returns every year as seasonal mood disorder.

5. **Bipolar disorder** is different from depression, but it is included in this list because someone with bipolar disorder experiences episodes of extremely low moods that meet the criteria for major depression (called 'bipolar depression'). But a person with bipolar disorder also experiences extreme high – euphoric or irritable – moods called 'mania' or a less severe form called 'hypomania.' These subtypes of manic depressive illness are Bipolar I Disorder and Bipolar II Disorder.

6. **Disruptive Mood Dysregulation Disorder** (DMDD) is a childhood condition (18 years and younger) of extreme irritability, anger, and frequent, intense temper outbursts. DMDD symptoms go beyond being a 'moody' child—children with DMDD experience severe impairment that requires clinical attention. This is the substitute Bipolar Disorder in children.

7. **Premenstrual Syndrome** (PMS) refers to a wide range of symptoms that start during the second half of the menstrual cycle (14 or more days after the first day of your last menstrual period) and ends one to two days after the menstrual period starts. PMS symptoms may be affective and physical, but they do not significantly impair job and social functioning.

8. **Premenstrual Dysphoric Disorder** (PMDD) is a condition in which a woman has severe depression symptoms, anxiety, irritability, and tension the week before menstruation. The symptoms of PMDD are more severe than those seen with premenstrual syndrome. They inhibit engaging in work, interpersonal relationships and other social activities. It is also called late luteal phase dysphoric disorder.

9. **Situational Depression** is a short-term form of depression that can occur in the aftermath of various traumatic changes in your normal life, including divorce, retirement, loss of a job and the death of a relative or close friend. Doctors sometimes refer to the condition as one of the stress-response syndromes of adjustment disorders. Systemic racism leads to chronic adjustment disorder in African Americans.

10. **Atypical Depression** is a subtype of major depression or dysthymic disorder that involves several specific symptoms, including increased appetite or weight gain, sleepiness or excessive sleep, marked fatigue or weakness, moods that are strongly reactive to environmental circumstances, and feeling extremely sensitive to rejection.

Why Does Depression Occur?[16]

Life events

"Research suggests that continuing difficulties -- long-term unemployment, living in an abusive or uncaring relationship, long-term isolation or loneliness, prolonged work stress -- are more likely to cause depression than recent life stresses. However, recent events (such as losing your job) or a combination of events can trigger depression if you're already at risk because of previous bad experiences or personal factors.

Personal factors

- Family history – Depression can run in families and some people will be at an increased genetic risk. However, having a parent or close relative with depression doesn't mean you'll

---

[16] What causes depression? (n.d.). Retrieved from Beyond Blue: https://www.beyondblue.org.au/the-facts/depression/what-causes- depression

automatically have the same experience. Life circumstances and other personal factors are still likely to have an important influence.

- Personality – Some people may be more at risk of depression because of their personality, particularly if they have a tendency to worry a lot, have low self-esteem, are perfectionists, are sensitive to personal criticism, or are self-critical and negative.

- Serious medical illness – The stress and worry of coping with a serious illness can lead to depression, especially if you're dealing with long-term management and/or chronic pain.

- Drug and alcohol use – Drug and alcohol use can both lead to and result from depression. Many people with depression also have drug and alcohol problems.

- Environmental perception – The environment impacts a person's response to stimuli in the ecosystem based on gradients of trust and control within the individual.

Based on our presentation, we now believe and understand how depression has been fueled and sustained in the African American community," the group leader continued. "When we considered the fact that depression can run in families and that some can be at an increased genetic risk, we found the correlation between enslavement, slave trauma and current rates of depression among African Americans undeniable.

"One of our proposed treatments for depression in this particular community is the acknowledgement of familial trauma. Just as mental health experts consider family history when diagnosing individuals, they should also consider family lineage of trauma, if it is known. As a group, we are of the belief that those traumatic experiences can be 'passed down' emotionally and spiritually. Although we don't have the expertise or knowledge to explain that belief, there are many doctors, scholars and historians who may be able to try. Perhaps we can scientifically prove, either genetically or psychologically, that traumatic memories and emotions (including those experienced by slaves) can be shared among generations. That would be a first step in expanding our current understanding of depression."

The group ended their presentation with an informative question and answer session. It was excellent.

"I am so proud of the work you have demonstrated thus far today," Professor Johnson chimed in. "I believe that we're in for another treat with the group three presentation."

"You're absolutely correct!" the group leader noted. "Our topic for this session is alcoholism, and we've chosen to present a case study for our collective discussion. We need your help identifying contributing factors, symptoms and possible solutions for the case. Let's take a look:

> Donna is a 37-year-old black woman who is divorced with two children. She has a steady but low paying retail job, and she supplements her income with welfare benefits such as food stamps and housing assistance. Although she grew up in a home with an alcoholic father, Donna did not take her first drink until she was 25. She started drinking socially on occasions, but began consuming wine and liquor more frequently after the birth of her second child and subsequent divorce from her husband.

Now, Donna drinks almost every night of the week. There are liquor stores on every corner of her neighborhood, and it is easy for Donna to get alcohol—as she usually trades some of her food stamps for one or two bottles. Donna usually blacks out at least once a week, and her kids have to call their uncles to come over and 'wake mommy up.'

Donna's family has suggested that she go to Alcoholics Anonymous for help, but Donna insists that she does not have a problem and only likes to drink to relieve a bit of stress at the end of heavy work days. She saw her father abuse alcohol—resulting in raging fits of anger—and she insists that her situation is not that bad. Plus, he drank a lot of malt liquor which she doesn't like.

"Before we open this up for a group discussion, we have some interesting postulates to share with you regarding alcohol use in the black community:

- African Americans tend to initiate drinking at much later ages than whites.
- African Americans report lower rates of alcohol use than whites.
- African Americans report lower levels of use in nearly all age groups.
- Yet, African Americans experience higher levels of alcohol abuse compared to whites

"Some of us may already be aware that there is a stigma in the black community surrounding alcohol. Socially and spiritually, we tend not to condone it which explains why initiation ages of alcohol consumption for Blacks are later than whites. This helps explain why Donna had her first drink at 25. Now, what do you think are some contributing factors to Donna's situation? Let's talk about the social and economic factors which may be relevant here, if any. "Donna seems to be experiencing higher levels of stress due to the birth of her baby and her divorce," a student responded.

"Yea, and she has a low-paying job and is on welfare. She might be having a hard time making ends meet," another student chimed in.

"She definitely has easy access to alcohol, which makes her habit easy to support," a third stated.

"Correct," the group leader added. "Studies have shown that very low income African Americans (especially men) are at the highest risk of alcohol abuse, and that makes sense due to the stress and pressure that comes along with that reality. Now, what are some of the symptoms that Donna is exhibiting? Remember, we are not doctors, and we are not professionally trained to diagnose Donna, but we can discuss our observations based on what we know and may have experienced."

"Well, it seems like the frequency at which Donna drinks is the most telling sign that she has an alcohol problem, although the study does not detail how much she's drinking every day. She is blacking out often, so she must be drinking a lot," a student suggested.

"And, she's in denial. She may not understand alcoholism if she's using her father as the model. She thinks that malt liquor is the only culprit," another added.

"We agree," a group member said. The group leader added,

"Although we can't officially diagnose Donna, we would recommend that she see a trained professional for counseling. That would be a great starting point for recovery. Other solutions we thought about include meditation, fellowship, and physical activities. Those things could help relieve some of Donna's stress and provide an alternative to drinking. Thank you all for your contributions to this discussion!"

The class responded with a warm applause. "Next up!" shouted Professor Johnson. "We are on a roll, folks—let's keep this train moving."

"Good morning class," said group four's leader. "Group three gave an excellent presentation, kudos to them—clap, clap! They are a tough act to follow, but we can handle it," she laughed. "Like group three, we are going to present a case study which we will simply call a short story."

Someone in group three shouted, "Copy cats!"

The group leader chided, "Don't you know that imitation is flattery? Here's our story:

> Jack is a 50-year-old African American. He is a college graduate, an engineer with a good job and works at the navy ship yard. He is married to a school teacher. They have two teenage sons in the local middle school where their mother teaches. They are a happy, middle class family.
>
> Jack started smoking weed and coming home late and high- smelling like what his wife called 'stale night club, day old cigarette butt

smoke.' She cautioned him that his behavior had to stop for the sake of the children. But it didn't. This went on for at least a year. He stopped paying the mortgage, then some of the bills. Household finances dwindled slowly, and he started taking money out of the savings account.

Meanwhile, his wife was busy 'robbing Peter to pay Paul'. She even took a second part-time job. They argued all the time and began sleeping in separate bedrooms. Most of the time, Jack was in another world. He lost weight, didn't eat and sometimes didn't even come home. He lost his job and didn't tell anyone. He started selling things from their home: silver, crystal, his wife's jewelry and other things. One day he was trying to play basketball with his sons and one of them noticed marks on his arms.

The son asked, 'What are those marks on your arms, dad?'

The other son, who was seemingly in shock, said, 'Dad, what is this? Man, don't tell me it's drugs!'

Jack, ashamed and speechless, dropped down to his knees and began to cry. The boys dropped down beside him and the three of them cried together.

"This is the story of substance abuse out of control. Can any of you relate to this story or share a similar drug-related one? What's going on in your neighborhood? In schools? In suburbs? What is the latest drug craze? What is the legal system doing? Mental health clinics? How about schools, churches, and community-based organizations? Drugs have gotten out of hand and reached an epidemic stage. Let's talk about it! Let's help do something about it. The floor is open for your comments. We thank you."

The discussion that followed was electrifying! The bell rang for the class to end while the students were still sharing stories. Professor Johnson told them that they would revisit substance abuse during the next class.

Substance Abuse

Dr. Johnson began the discussion by pointing out that experts and practitioners in the field use the term "substance abuse disorders" instead of "substance abuse" and "substance dependence." According to Substance Abuse and Mental Health Services Administration (SAMHSA), substance use disorders occur when the recurrent use of alcohol and or drugs causes clinically and functionally significant impairment such as health problems, disability and failure to meet major responsibilities at work, school, or home.[17] Because of the rapid increase in drug use and availability, it is important for us to understand some of the major substance abuse disorders. He began the discussion with two questions:

1. "Do you know anyone who suffers from any kind of substance abuse disorder?

2. What are some general symptoms or characteristics of substance abuse disorders?"

He then wrote three categories of changes that substance users undergo: behavioral changes, physical changes, and social changes. As the students discussed various symptoms, Dr. Johnson recorded

---

[17] Substance Use Disorders. (2015, October 27). Retrieved from Substance Abuse and Mental Health Services Administration: http://www.samhsa.gov/disorders/substance-use

them on the white board.[18]

Behavioral changes:

- Drop in attendance and performance at work or school
- Frequently getting into trouble (fights, accidents, illegal activities)
- Using substances in physically hazardous situations such as while driving or operating a machine
- Engaging in secretive or suspicious behaviors
- Changes in appetite or sleep patterns
- Unexplained change in personality or attitude
- Sudden mood swings, irritability, or angry outbursts
- Periods of unusual hyperactivity, agitation, or giddiness
- Lacking motivation
- Appearing fearful, anxious, or paranoid, with no reason

Physical changes:

- Bloodshot eyes and abnormally sized pupils
- Sudden weight loss or weight gain
- Deterioration of physical appearance
- Unusual smells on breath, body, or clothing
- Tremors, slurred speech, or impaired coordination

---

[18] Mental Health and Substance Use Disorders. (n.d.). Retrieved from U.S. Department of Health & Human Services: https://www.mentalhealth.gov/what-to-look-for/substance- abuse/index.html

Social changes:

- Sudden change in friends, favorite hangouts, and hobbies
- Legal problems related to substance use
- Unexplained need for money or financial problems
- Using substances even though it causes problems in relationships

After discussing some general symptoms of substance use disorders, the class reviewed a handout with a detailed list and overview of the specific disorders.

Substance Use Disorders[19]

1. Alcohol dependence is a psychiatric diagnosis in which a person continues to use alcohol despite negative consequences to relationships, work or quality of health and life. Alcohol dependence includes both a physical and mental addiction to alcohol. This addiction can dominate all areas of life in a detrimental way, yet the affected person is unable to control or easily quit using alcohol.

   Symptoms:

   - Increased alcohol tolerance (needing more and more to become drunk)

---

[19] Alcohol Dependence. (n.d.). Retrieved from Allaboutcounseling.com: www.allaboutcounseling.com/library/alcohol-dependence

- Withdrawal when alcohol use is stopped
- Continuous drinking, despite harm to health, relationships, and jobs
- Drinking alone (not just social situations)
- Violent behaviors when drunk
- Denial and irritation when confronted about a drinking problem
- Making excuses
- Ending participation in regular activities
- Neglecting appearance, health, and diet
- Attempt to hide drinking

2. Amphetamine dependence: Amphetamines are a group of powerful and highly addictive drugs that come in a variety of forms and nicknames. Amphetamines are also known as sympathomimetics, stimulants, and psychostimulants. The most common illegally produced amphetamine, methamphetamine, goes by the street name of "speed," "meth," and "chalk." When it is smoked, it is called "ice," "crystal," "crank," and "glass." They induce feelings of well-being and improve alertness and attention. Because the substance is highly addictive, amphetamine users need more and more, and can quickly lose control and fall into amphetamine dependence. Chronic, heavy use of amphetamines is very serious, and even changes the molecular make up and functioning of the brain. Over a period of time, the initial feelings of well-being turn into feelings of panic, depression and thoughts of suicide.

Symptoms:

- Compulsive seeking of amphetamines
- Aggressive or violent behavior when using or seeking amphetamines
- Anxiety and panic
- Paranoid behavior
- Psychotic episodes similar to schizophrenia
- Hallucinations
- Delusions
- Hyperactivity and hypersexuality
- Confusion, incoherence
- Negative effects in relationships, work, and school
- Thoughts of suicide
- Depression

3. Cannabis dependence: Cannabis, more commonly known as marijuana, is considered the most commonly used illegal substance in the world. Cannabis dependence is a problem that has psychiatric implications and therefore is a psychiatric diagnosis. To many people, cannabis seems relatively harmless even with prolonged use. After all, it does help people with chronic pain, including pain from certain cancers. While cannabis does have appropriate medical uses and is used recreationally by many, it can cause problems in personal relationships, work, school and personal health.

Symptoms:

- Compulsive seeking and use of cannabis
- Tolerance of effects, requiring more and more to feel high
- Symptoms of withdrawal upon quitting use
- Respiratory problems like chronic bronchitis
- Damage to lung tissue
- Increase in heart rate and blood pressure (especially if cannabis is combined with another drug such as cocaine)
- Impaired memory and learning skills
- Negative effects in family, relationships, work and school
- Legal problems related to cannabis
- Desire to quit use, with failed attempts

4. Cocaine dependence: Cocaine dependence is a serious problem that has psychiatric and psychological implications. Cocaine dependence, also known as addiction, is much more severe and serious than cocaine use or abuse. Dependence is a maladaptive behavior that, over a three-month period, has caused the affected individual to experience tolerance for and withdrawal symptoms from cocaine. Dependence comes with a lot of other problems that negatively affect all aspects of life from health, to personal relationships, to the ability to keep a job, and so on. It can also cause heart, brain, and nerve damage and a variety of serious mood disorders.

Symptoms:

- Compulsive seeking and usage of cocaine

- Increased tolerance to its effects
- Symptoms of withdrawal upon quitting
- Depression
- Irritability and agitation
- Lack of motivation
- Sleeping problems
- Anxiety and panic attacks
- Hallucinations
- Psychosis
- Drastic personality changes

5. Hallucinogen dependence: Hallucinogens are a large and varied group of drugs that alter a person's perception, consciousness, mood and thinking. Hallucinogenic drugs can be divided into three basic categories including psychedelics, dissociatives and deliriants. These drugs are generally used recreationally, or sometimes for spiritual or religious purposes as seen in the use of peyote among indigenous people of the Americas. Hallucinogens usually don't lead to addiction, but they can in certain individuals. Negative effects of prolonged hallucinogens use can cause health problems, mood disorders, and many problems in personal life including relationships, work and so on.

Symptoms:

- Confusion, delusions and paranoia
- Anxiety attacks and panic
- Flashbacks after the drug is out of the body

- Impaired concentration and motivation
- Long-term memory loss
- Personality changes
- Increased blood pressure and heart rate
- Blurred vision
- Poor coordination
- Restlessness
- Seizures
- Diarrhea, sweating, cramping and dehydration
- Negative effects to relationships, jobs and family life

6. Inhalant dependence: It is not uncommon for someone to use an inhaler as medication for breathing conditions, such as asthma. Those who have asthma know what it is like to use an inhaler so that they may breathe easier. It is dangerous, however, to inhale substances that are not for medical use, such as glue, gasoline or more risky drugs. Many people may think that inhaling such substances is harmless, but there are many consequences and complications that may arise.

People who have an inhalant dependence continue to use inhalants even though they are aware of the problems that are caused by or made worse by the use of the substance. The inhalants are a class of drugs that include a wide range of chemicals that are found in hundreds of different products. Most inhalants are readily available to the general population. Chemicals that are inhaled include liquids that vaporize at room temperature and aerosols (e.g., glue, gasoline, paint thinner, hair spray, nail polish, lighter fluid, and paint thinner). Inhalants can be sniffed directly from the container by inhaling fumes from a bag or by inhaling the substance from a cloth soaked in it.

Symptoms:

- Building a tolerance to the substance
- Failing to stop using even if desired
- Losing of control and repeatedly using the substance longer than planned
- Giving up social activities or sports to use the substance
- Using the substance even when developing psychological or physical problems

7. Nicotine dependence: Nicotine dependence and addiction has been one of the hardest addictions to break. Nicotine dependence occurs when someone has a physical addiction to the chemical nicotine, which is commonly delivered in various tobacco products, such as cigars, cigarettes, pipes and chewing tobacco. There is not a type of tobacco that is safe to use. Nicotine is a very addictive drug that causes changes in the brain that make you crave more.

Symptoms:

- Desiring more of the drug
- Not being able to stop taking the drug
- Having to take the drug just to get through the day
- Difficulty concentrating

- Restlessness

8. Opioid dependence: Opioids are narcotic pain relievers that work by changing the way the brain receives pain. They are commonly prescribed by doctors to relieve mild to severe pain. Codeine, Morphine, OxyContin, Darvon, Demerol, Vicodin and Diluadad are commonly known opioids. They work by attaching to specific proteins in the brain, spinal cord and gastrointestinal tract, and block the transmission of pain messages to the brain. Opioids also change the way our brain perceives pain. They can produce drowsiness and euphoria by affecting the brain regions that produce pleasure.

    Symptoms:

    - Restlessness
    - Muscle and bone pain
    - Insomnia
    - Diarrhea
    - Vomiting
    - Cold flashes
    - Involuntary leg movements

9. Phencyclidine dependence: Phencyclidine, more commonly known as PCP, was originally developed in the 1950s as an intravenous anesthetic, but has been discontinued due to serious side effects. However, PCP is often sold on the illegal drug market in various forms, and it can be mixed easily with dyes. Tablets, capsules and colored powder are

the forms that are most commonly sold, as they can be snorted, smoked or orally ingested. Other hallucinogens that are similar to PCP are LSD, Peyote and Psilocybin. Research suggests that these drugs work by temporarily interfering with neurotransmitter action or by binding to their receptor sites. PCP distorts perceptions of sight and sound and produces feelings of detachment from the environment and self. The effects of PCP usually last between four to six hours.

Symptoms:

- Memory loss
- Hallucinations
- Paranoia
- Delusions
- Loss of balance
- Dizziness
- Loss of muscle control
- Blurred vision

10. Sedative dependence: Sedatives are commonly used in conjunction with surgery and are prescribed by doctors to treat pain, anxiety, panic attacks and insomnia. If used properly, sedatives can be beneficial; however, many people misuse these drugs, which may lead to abuse, dependence and withdrawal.

Sedatives are compounds that cause physiological and mental slowing of the body. They are often referred to as tranquilizers, as they work by increasing the amount of the neurotransmitter gamma-aminobutyric acid (GABA) in the brain. These neurotransmitters help regulate the speed of nerve impulses.

Sedatives reduce pain, anxiety and causes sleepiness and muscle relaxation. The most widely prescribed sedatives belong to a group called benzodiazepines, which include drugs such as Xanax, Librium, Ambien, Valium and Tranxene.

Symptoms:

- Actively seeking sedatives in multiple places
- Going to several doctors in order to obtain multiple prescriptions
- Continued use of sedatives despite health problems
- Finding and needing a sedative just to function
- Nausea
- Insomnia
- Sweating
- Hypertension

The students shared stories about friends who experimented with drugs and got hooked, guys who became dealers and pushers, girls who became addicts and walked the streets at night, men and women who committed crimes and, in short, "messed their lives up."

This was an exciting class; however, there was not enough time for all of the feedback that the students wanted to give. So, Dr. Johnson dismissed the class as scheduled. He reminded them about the upcoming Executive Leadership Forum with an extraordinary group of scholars, researchers and authors who would address substance use disorders, prevention, and plausible solutions.

PART III
Miseducation

Miseducation

How shameful that men of influence should mislead and miseducate the public mind.

\- *American Eloquence* Volume IV

D r. Johnson's energy and the high spirits of his students sometimes drained him. He put a lot into his classes to keep students engaged and motivated. His classes were lively and fast-paced. This evening, however, he couldn't wait to go home and "chillax." All he wanted to do was spend some time with Mildred—maybe go to a quiet restaurant for a romantic dinner.

"Great idea," he said to himself, "then we can come home, and snuggle up for some Tender Loving Care (TLC)."

When he arrived home, it was almost as if some mental telepathy had taken place.

"Good evening Honey," Mildred said as she gave him a kiss on the cheek.

"Hey baby," John replied.

"Honey, can we go someplace for a quiet dinner? I really need to wind down and chill," Mildred said.

"I had that same thought as I left the campus. How soon can you be ready, Babe?" he replied.

"Give me ten minutes and I'll be good to go," she said to John. Thereafter, they left for the Mesob Café which was one of their favorite restaurants.

The Mesob Café specializes in Ethiopian and Eritrean cuisine. John and Mildred ordered Doro Wot, a chicken stew served with hard-boiled eggs, and Gomen, collard greens cooked with onions and jalapenos, for dinner. Mildred was always interested in John's classes and his students. And tonight, John talked more than usual about how things were going.

"Honey, what's the lesson plan for your class tomorrow?" Mildred asked as they enjoyed their meal.

John replied, "We are going to discuss miseducation."

Mildred said, "That's going to be a good class. I love Carter G. Woodson's works, and I often share his philosophy and quotes when I speak to youth and young adults. Do you remember the quote which says: 'When you control a man's thinking, you do not have to worry about his actions. You do not have to tell him to stand here or go yonder. He will find his 'proper place' and will stay in it. You do not need to send him to the back door. He will go without being told. In fact, if there is no back door, he will cut one for his special benefit. His education makes it necessary as he explains in his book, *The Miseducation of the Negro*."

"I sure do, Babe. I am going to talk about that as part of my lecture tomorrow," he said.

"Honey, will you explain more about your approach towards and treatment of miseducation? Will his book, *The Miseducation of the Negro*, be your major focus?" Mildred asked.

"That's a good question," John said. "Here's my plan: I postulate that miseducation has been and remains a widespread problem that needs to be addressed from diverse perspectives. My lecture will provide a retrospective commentary relating to three historical contexts:

1. Miseducation of Africa (Roots and Egypt on the Potomac)
2. Miseducation of the Negro (Carter G. Woodson)
3. Miseducation of African Americans today

"Do you want to read my discussion notes?"

"I thought that you would never ask! I'd love to," Mildred replied.

John said, "That's great, Babe, but let's not talk any more academics for now. Let's enjoy some bunna (hot coffee) and tiramisu to top off our wonderful dinner, OK?"

"I'll co-sign that," Mildred chuckled as John signaled for the waitress.

Dinner was excellent. John and Mildred had a wonderful evening. They left the Mesob Café relaxed and happy; they smiled and hugged as Mildred hummed the song, "Tomorrow." ("The sun will come out tomorrow…").

When tomorrow came, John was ecstatic. He arrived at his class early in order to prepare his PowerPoint and handouts for the day. He reserved a few seats at the front of the class for the grandchildren, who Grandma Johnson had promised to bring by after school. He wanted to make sure that they were able to participate in the class discussion, even if they were not quite old enough to fully understand the concept of miseducation. At least they will be introduced to some new information, which has the capacity to change their perspectives and their lives in ways that are essential to their full development. This could change their world. He smiled.

Around 2:50 pm, the class began to file in and take their seats. At 2:59 pm, the grandchildren ran in, excited and anxious to be around college students in a big classroom. At 3:00 pm sharp, Professor Johnson greeted his students and introduced Jeannie, Sandra and Keith to the class. He turned, and in big letters, wrote the following word on the chalkboard:

MISEDUCATION

"This is a class session which I have yearned to teach for many years," Professor Johnson started. "You will not find this class in the majority of our universities throughout the United States, and where they do exist, you are likely to only find them listed as African studies classes. I personally know a few professors who, many years ago, were fired for attempting to teach the things which we are to discuss today. I pray that you would keep your minds open and, for the duration of the class, set aside any knowledge that you have deemed as 'fact' regarding African or black history. I ask that you allow me to present some things to you, even though they might surprise or challenge the things you grew up learning. If you can do that, I believe that we will grow together. Is that all right?"

The class seemed eager to get started.

Professor Johnson continued, "Miseducation, in its simplest definition, is improper, wrong, or deficient teaching. The term 'miseducation' offends some people, but it's usually the people who are on the side of the wrong or deficient teaching. Now, you can take nearly any discipline or field and find a good amount of miseducation operating there, but I firmly believe that nowhere is miseducation more widespread and problematic than that within the black community. From cradle to grave, African Americans are given extremely high dosages of misinformation about their past, their present and their future. There are some interesting reasons why, and we are going to talk about that today.

I've divided the class into three segments in order for us to dissect three stories or concepts which have risen to prominence about the black community, and we will discuss why these stories are forms of miseducation as well as the impact of such deceit."

Professor Johnson dimmed the lights and started his PowerPoint. The first slide showed two images side-by-side. They were family trees. The image on the left showed an elaborate tree with many branches and European-looking names written on them. There were at least seven generations depicted on the tree. The image on the right depicted the same tree, except only four generations of names were written on the branches. The majority of the boxes for names to be written were empty, and the tree looked starkly in comparison to the one on the left.

Keith, the oldest grandchild, suddenly blurted out, "Hey, Uncle John—we did one of those trees for my class last year! You helped me with it, remember? Mine looked like the one on the right. I couldn't fill in that many boxes. But some of my friends had a lot of names up there, like the tree on the left. They even brought in photos of their great-great-grandparents and everything."

"I sure do remember, Keith," Uncle John replied. "I've thought about that tree a lot since we made it. Did you know that the deeper a tree's roots go, the higher and taller it will grow? On paper, it looks like we don't have a large family and so our tree looks stunted. It looks like our roots don't go that far down. Many people have used this visual to convey a certain message to African Americans, but this is an instance where the proof is not on the paper. We can't always believe what we see."

Myth #1: The Black Man Has No History or Heritage

Shifting his attention to the class, Professor Johnson continued, "The first concept that I want to debunk today is this: The black man has no history or heritage. A visit to a modern third or fourth grade classroom in America will have one believe that this is true. In most elementary textbooks, the story of the African American begins at the point of his departure from Africa, in chains, with little to no mention of the captured village, country or culture. The most we are told, with no context or explanation, is that Africans enslaved other Africans. A few people decided, long ago, that it was as much as our elementary-aged children needed to know about African history. The rest would have to be acquired, optionally, in high school or college. At the same time, we are extensively taught about the histories and heritage of European nations, the founding of America, and the like."

"Isn't there a name for that?" one of the students chimed in.

"Yea—it's called whitewashing," another responded. Others nodded in agreement.

"Indeed!" Professor Johnson replied. "For some specific reasons, our culture has chosen to glorify the white experience and minimize the black experience, simultaneously stigmatizing those who desire to learn or teach the truth about African history and culture. Could you imagine the shock and awe that many would experience to learn the following:[20]

- Few people talk about the early Africans who sailed to America centuries before Columbus did; however, Columbus himself journaled that the Native Americans confirmed 'black-skinned people had come from the southeast in boats, trading in gold-tipped spears.'

- Archaeologists have recently discovered American narcotics in Egyptian mummies, including South American cocaine and nicotine.

- Egyptian artifacts and hieroglyphics have been found in North America, specifically in the Grand Canyon. It's interesting to note here that the National Park Service will not allow archaeologists to excavate any of the pyramids in the Grand Canyon.

- Skulls and skeletons belonging to people of African descent have been discovered in the Americas.

- Other European explorers, including Vasco Nunez de Balboa, recorded seeing 'Negroes' in the new world.

"In fact, it is documented that black Egyptians were sailing to the Americas as early as 1292 B.C. during King Ramses III's reign." He paused for a moment. "Who among you has heard of the Olmec civilization of ancient Mexico? Considered the first

---

[20] Gordon, T. (2015, January 23). 10 Pieces of Evidence That Prove Black People Sailed to the Americas Long Before Columbus. Retrieved from Atlanta Black Star: http://atlantablackstar.com/2015/01/23/10-pieces-of-evidence-that- prove-black-people-sailed-to-the-americas-long-before-columbus/

advanced civilization of the Americas, some believe that they were of African origin based on the large stone heads that were discovered and depict African features.

"We can look no further than our nation Capital to find African inspired symbols, monuments and designs on display. The Washington Monument, for instance, was designed to replicate an Egyptian obelisk, a structure which has been replicated many times throughout the world and fascinates many to this day. In local architecture throughout the city, Egyptian designs and features are repeated and remodeled. It is clear that the developers of the Capital were fascinated and inspired by African design and culture.[21] We just don't hear that much about it.

"Furthermore, we don't hear about African Americans like Benjamin Banneker, who was a part of the team that surveyed the city before it was built. More credit is given to men like Pierre Charles L'Enfant, who quit the project, while Banneker carried on. And today, most people walk through the streets of the nation Capital having no idea of the contributions made by Africans and African Americans. Educator Anthony T. Browder has an excellent book on the subject called *Egypt on the Potomac: A Guide to Decoding Egyptian Architecture and Symbolism in Washington, D.C.*"

The class sat in awe as Professor Johnson displayed images to back up his points. Many just shook their heads and took notes.

"Now, let's explain these stories. Why do you think that so many

---

[21] Anthony T. Browder- Egypt on the Potomac Field Trip (2014). [Motion Picture].

like them are untold today? What is the benefit of erasing this history and heritage?", Professor Johnson asked.

A student replied, "It's evident that African slaves were forced into this country for one reason—labor. In order for the labor to be effective, for control to be established and maintained, for a new order to be determined, then histories, accomplishments and achievements would have to be minimized. Who cares about teaching a man his history when all you need out of him is his back? You don't need his mind, and you certainly don't need his self-awareness."

"Absolutely," a second student added. "Knowledge breeds awareness, identity, and confidence. Those three things would have been the greatest threats to slave owners and those benefitting from the system of slavery."

"With so many families separated and mixed with those of other cultures, it's amazing that any history was preserved among the slaves. It would have been left to individuals or small groups to remember those things and pass them down to their children, so I understand how stories and histories could easily get lost after one or two generations," a third student remarked.

"Very good input," Professor Johnson said. "What intrigues me most is why the narrative that African Americans have no history or heritage is still propagated today. We no longer force slave labor. So, what's the threat of African Americans knowing their own history?"

A fourth student said, "I believe that there is a lack of those who are dedicated to discovering the truth. I don't know for sure, but I would bet that Blacks are not studying archaeology and anthropology at the same rates that other cultures are. We need more people who are bold enough to present alternative viewpoints and teach the masses. There are some voices but not many, like Dr. Yosef Ben-Jochannan, who have dug deep to research and show what the true history is. They've visited the great libraries and monuments, studied ancient texts, learned the ancient languages, and they've returned with puzzle pieces that they've put together in front of us to make those connections. Too few are following in their footsteps."

"I agree," another replied. "I think it's human nature for cultures to be self-centered. European history is one of dominance and image. So many customs, practices, arts, technologies have been credited to and by Europeans after they learned them from other cultures. If certain truths were revealed, then those accomplishments and entitlements would be stripped away, essentially stripping away the perceived identity of its people and its descendants."

"Now," Professor Johnson added, "imagine if that same sense of accomplishment and identity were given to its rightful owners? What if African Americans were aware of the accomplishments and histories of their ancestors? I think that would change everything. When we know what we've done, then we know what we're capable of doing. We know who we are. Our roots begin to grow deeper, our foundation is stronger, and our branches begin to grow. A generation of children who is failing and dropping out of school would turn into one who is hopeful and proud, propelled by the success and contributions of its family tree.

"There is really no way to statistically or numerically measure the impact that this type of miseducation has had on African Americans. But we can commit to do better moving forward. That's why I have my nieces and nephew here with us today. Let's break and return for our second segment of the class in a few minutes."

Ten minutes later, the class was settled back into their seats and anxious to hear part two of Professor Johnson's lecture. Again, Professor Johnson dimmed the lights and resourced his PowerPoint. This time, he displayed a bright image of a colorful postcard from the 1900's. On it were two black men, drastically caricatured as monkeys, carelessly enjoying a cigar. Their skin was black, their lips large and bright red, and their white teeth protruded from their mouths.

Myth #2: The Black Man is Inferior, Subordinate and Subhuman

Professor Johnson explained: "The second concept of miseducation that I want to debunk today is this: The black man is inferior, subordinate and subhuman. This is a misconception that is evidenced by thousands of images like this one, easily found on the Internet today. It suggests that Africans and African Americans are inherently less intelligent than, less developed than, and less human than whites. It purports that Africans and African Americans are brutes, instinctual savages who resemble monkeys both physically and developmentally. It is one of the longest-running misconceptions that this world has ever seen, spanning centuries and continents.

"This misconception has fueled scientific research, academic debate and even mass entertainment since before slavery, and it has yet to stop. It has affected the African, the enslaved Negro and today's African American in subliminal and irreversible ways. I'd like to start examining this second concept by making the statement more specific and focused: The African is inferior, subordinate and subhuman.

"Historically, there were countless men and women who truly believed that Africans were racially inferior to whites, and they spread racist and ludicrous theories which became popular and accepted ideologies at one point. Among them was English theorist Sir William Petty, who described a hierarchal pyramid in his manuscript, *Scale of Creatures* that ranked God's creatures from greatest to least. Caucasians, portrayed by Petty as the original race of man, were at the top of the pyramid while Negroes fell towards the bottom as 'the most beastlike of all the souls' and closest to apes and lesser creatures. This theory was used, in part, to justify the trans-Atlantic slave trade. [22]

"Two centuries later, another theorist named Sir Francis Galton ranked the mental capacities of various ethnic groups and presented them in a chapter titled "The Comparative Worth of Different Races" in his 1869 book called *Hereditary Genius*. He purported that people of African descent were two grades lower

---

[22] Scott, T. (2014, December 26). 10 Racist Scientific Theories About Black People That Have Been Thoroughly Debunked. Retrieved from Atlanta Black Star: http://atlantablackstar.com/2014/12/26/10-racist-scientific-theories- about-black-people-that-has-been-thoroughly-debunked/

than Europeans. His theories and scientific techniques inspired the authors of the controversial *Bell Curve Theory*, Richard J. Herrnstein and Charles Murray.

"The most disturbing theory concerning the historical humaneness and intelligence of Africans is known as the Hamitic myth, which reasons that dark-skinned Caucasians called Hamites invaded and conquered Africans because of their superior wit. Hamites, then, were ultimately responsible for cultural, scientific and intellectual achievements in Africa. [23]

"At the height of slavery in the West, a similar yet newly focused concept emerged: The Negro slave is inferior, subordinate and subhuman.

"Consider Samuel A. Cartwright, a 19th century physician who coined the term 'Drapetomania' to describe the mental disease which spirited some black slaves, who he considered naturally submissive and lacking in self-determination, to become defiant and escape from their masters. Cartwright's proposed treatment for this disorder was to whip the devil out of them. Like pets, Negros needed to be tamed, ruled over and cared for.[24]

"Similarly, American physician Josiah Clark Nott asserted a defensive stance in regard to slavery through polygenic claims and studies. He was a notable follower of Samuel George Morton, who was among the first to claim that intellectual

---

[23] Sachsen-Gotha, S. (2014, November 24). 10 Racist Scientific Theories that Changed the World. Retrieved from Listverse: http://listverse.com/2014/11/24/ten-racist-scientific-theories-that-changed-the-world/
[24] See: Racism & Psychiatry by Audrey Thomas and Samuel Sillen

capacity could be judged by cranial capacity. Nott took Morton's ideas a step further in his 1854 work, *Types of Mankind*. Like many other polygenists, Nott believed that Negros were inferior, even claiming that the Negro achieves his greatest perfection, physical and moral, and also greatest longevity, in a state of slavery.[25]

"Today, an eerily similar yet even more focused concept is emerging and continues to pervade our nation's conscience: The African American is inferior, subordinate and subhuman. Believe it or not, scientific racism still exists today, such as in the fairly recent work of Richard Herrnstein and Charles Murray. Their 1994 book, *The Bell Curve: Intelligence and Class in American Life*, argues that IQ is the dominant factor in determining the economic and social class differences between blacks and whites. Most controversial among the authors' claims is that the poor and unfortunate are simply not as intelligent as the wealthy, known as the 'cognitive elite,' followed by statistical data supporting the claim that blacks were less intelligent than whites.[26]

"Moving away from science for a moment, we can even see this concept propagated in mainstream media. In 2011, the Opportunity Agenda published a Social Science Literature Review titled, *Media Representations and Impact on the Lives of Black Men and Boys* throughout which they presented and explained the following distorted patterns of portrayal of black men in media: underrepresentation overall; negative associations exaggerated; positive associations limited; the 'problem' frame; and missing

---

[25] Dewbury, Adam, "The American School and Scientific Racism in Early American Anthropology"/ in Darnell, Regna; Gleach, Frederic W., *Histories of Anthropology Annual*, 3, p. 142

[26] Charles Murray. (n.d.). Retrieved from Southern Poverty Law Center: https://www.splcenter.org/fighting-hate/extremist- files/individual/charles-murray

stories.[27] Aren't the consistent portrayals of blacks as criminals, housemaids, 'drug users', prostitutes and gangsters overplayed, and don't they connote black inferiority overall?

"Collectively, these polygenic, racist ideas were birthed during an era, shortly after the discovery of the wonders of Egypt by Napoleon and the development of modern science in the 18th century, in which man sought to order and classify his world while staking his claim in it. The ranking and classification of the races could help to establish and cement dominance, and Europeans assumed the highest rank. They particularly wanted credit for the achievements and wonders of the Egyptian civilization, which they fought to explain, through scientific racism, as creations of the Caucasian race while simultaneously explaining away the African features and portrayals throughout Egypt.

"Together, these concepts were widely spread and accepted as forms of miseducation despite theories and facts which attempted to demonstrate otherwise. There are numerous reasons why, but I do not want to get ahead of myself. Before we discuss the explanation and effects of these extreme misconceptions, we must first discover the truth.

"Let's start with some history which combats the myth that Africans are inferior, subordinate, and subhuman. Perhaps one of the greatest, most intelligent and renowned Africans in history is

---

[27] Social Science Literature Review: Media Representations and Impact on the Lives of Black Men and Boys. (2011, October). Retrieved from The Opportunity Agenda: http://www.racialequitytools.org/resourcefiles/Media-Impact- onLives-of-Black-Men-and-Boys-OppAgenda.pdf

Imhotep, the Egyptian architect, advisor, physician and healer. Imhotep was chief architect to pharaoh Djoser who reigned from 2630-2611 B.C. and was responsible for the world's first known monumental stone building, the Step Pyramid at Sakkara.[28] His building would go on to influence architects around the world and throughout history. (For instance, today visitors to Washington, D.C. can see a version of the step pyramid located at 1733 16th Street, NW).

"Throughout Egypt he was known as a wise counselor and skilled physician, credited with treating diseases such as arthritis and appendicitis with medicine extracted from plants. Imhotep was glorified as a mediator between men and the gods, was served by his own priesthood, and was one of only two Egyptians to be fully deified. After the Greeks conquered Egypt, the natives continued to worship and build temples to him; he remained renowned until the Arab invasion of North Africa. Here are some quick facts and figures regarding Imhotep that you should know:[29]

- Imhotep's Step Pyramid was the first monument made of stone and rose 204 feet and was surrounded by a 30 foot wall and 2,460 foot trench. It contained a temple, courtyards, shrines and living quarters.
- Imhotep practiced medicine nearly 2,200 years before Hippocrates and is considered the author of the Edwin Smith Papyrus, which contains 100 anatomical terms and describes 48 injuries and their treatments.

---

[28] Imhotep. (n.d.). Retrieved from BBC:
http://www.bbc.co.uk/history/historic_figures/imhotep.shtml
[29] Mark, J. (2016, February 16). Imhotep. Retrieved from Ancient History Encyclopedia: http://www.ancient.eu/imhotep/

- Imhotep was born a commoner yet rose to prominence due to his intelligence and natural talent.
- His works were influential during the Roman Empire, and the emperors Claudius and Tiberius praised him with inscriptions in their temples.

"Now, does this African sound like a man who is inferior, subordinate, and subhuman to you? He is one of many Africans who contributed to the development of civilization, and growth of Africa and the world.

"Next, let's tackle the myth that Negro slaves were inferior, subordinate and subhuman. There was a man named Benjamin Bradley who was born into slavery in Maryland around 1830.[30] Bradley was put to work in a printing office where he intuitively created a steam engine using scrap metal. He eventually earned a job at the Annapolis Naval Academy as an assistant in the science department. There, he continued to work on his steam engine and created the first one large enough to drive the first steam-powered warship at 16 knots. Because he was a slave, Bradley was legally not allowed to patent his invention. He did eventually sell the engine and purchased his freedom.

"Another inventor by the name of Henry Boyd was born a slave in Kentucky in 1802.[31] Boyd was a carpenter, and he built the first corded bed, 'The Boyd Bedstead,' which contained wooden rails

---

[30] Tracy. (2014, February 11). 5 Inventions by Enslaved Black Men Blocked by US Patent Office. Retrieved from Atlanta Black Star: http://atlantablackstar.com/2014/02/11/5-inventions-by-enslaved-black- men-blocked-by-us-patent-office/3/
[31] Pasha. (2007, October 5). Henry Boyd- Black inventor. Retrieved from Each One Teach One: http://www.eachoneteachone.org.uk/henry-boyd/

that connected to the headboard and footboard for a firmer structure. This is a common bedding style today. Like Bradley, Boyd was also unable to secure a patent for his invention.

"These two men of genius, like many enslaved and free throughout antebellum America, existed, and they made undeniable contributions to our society. They confounded whites who could not believe or accept that Negroes were capable of such achievements; therefore, many were never acknowledged or credited for their ingenuity. Instead, they received criticism, doubt and refusal of rights to patent. Imagine how many Negroes invented, engineered, pioneered and created new things during slavery. Imagine the number of men and women whose contributions we will never hear about. It is believed, for example, that the practice of processing meat began on the Gwaltney Plantation by my very own ancestors, Professor Johnson stated.

"Perhaps one of the greatest misfortunes of slavery is that many of these records and acknowledgements simply do not exist. And, as we talked about a moment ago, if the record does not exist, then it is implied that the history itself does not exist.

"Could it be that to acknowledge these Negro creators and thinkers, it would force many whites to reconsider the notions that they were taught, incorrectly, that Blacks were inherently inferior and incapable of intelligent thinking? I believe so.

"Finally, let's debunk the myth that African Americans today are inferior, subordinate and subhuman, and I am eager to start in the realm of science. Despite centuries of racist scientists arguing for the superiority of whites solely on the basis of IQ and cranial capacity, scientists are recently concluding that there is no single measure of intelligence, and that the IQ number is not an accurate measurement of intellect.[32]

"In an April 2013 issue of the journal *Neuron*, a research team led by Adrian Owen and Adam Hampshire of The Brain and Mind Institute of Western University published an article, "Fractioning Human Intelligence". The article presented the findings of a landmark intelligence study including more than 100,000 global participants. Using a series of 12 cognitive tests, the team concluded that the individual IQ score is misleading because it does not account for multiple types of intelligence which impact different brain systems. Part of their study included an examination of social demographics which they expect correlate with different types of intelligence.[33]

"Adam Hampshire, who co-authored the article, notes, 'We often hear these comparisons (of intelligence) and it's a terrible oversimplification. People should be skeptical when they hear these reports of population differences in IQ; it shouldn't be a unitary measure. Examining the social demographic correlations in more detail will help to understand them better.'

"I agree with Hampshire and Owen that more research needs to be done in the realm of intelligence which considers more environmental factors. To present evidence of IQ superiority

[32] Talbot, A. (2013, May 7). Debunking the IQ Myth. Retrieved from American Renaissance: http://www.amren.com/news/2013/05/debunking-the-iq- myth/
[33] Talbot, A. (2013, May 7). Debunking the IQ Myth. Retrieved from American Renaissance: http://www.amren.com/news/2013/05/debunking-the-iq- myth/

without doing so is dangerous as its implications extend beyond the sciences and pervade social, cultural and communal attitudes.[34] "Here's another perspective from the late Dr. Frances Cress Welsing, the prominent black psychiatrist, whose theories you've heard mentioned in recent classes. Dr. Welsing challenged the notion of white superiority by considering a global view of color. In a 2013 lecture titled "Surviving Racism in the 21st Century," Dr. Welsing mentioned that the notion that whites are superior is simply false because they compose only 1/10th of the world's population, whereas people of color (black, brown and yellow) comprise 9/10ths of the world's population. Dr. Welsing postulated that once white explorers, encountering diverse colored populations around the world, discovered that interracial relationships produced brown babies, they began to fear the loss of their white complexion, recognizing that their pigmentation genes were recessive. In an attempt to preserve their race and ensure their genetic survival, an all-out attempt to control and dominate the black race ensued through an all-encompassing system which involved education, economics, entertainment, labor, law, politics, religion, sex, and war. This system, according to Welsing, remains to this day and involves the propagation of black inferiority as one of its primary weapons.[35]

"What Welsing begins to tug at is the 'why' of white superiority. Who and what does it profit for the myth of black inferiority to be proliferated at the rate and extent to which it has for the past several centuries? Because we've classified this as a three part

[34] Talbot, A. (2013, May 7). Debunking the IQ Myth. Retrieved from American Renaissance: http://www.amren.com/news/2013/05/debunking-the-iq- myth/
[35] Welsing, D. F. (2013, September 3). Surviving Racism in the 21st Century- Part I. Retrieved from YouTube: https://www.youtube.com/watch?v=ZdbIpa0AfuQ

problem, I believe there is a three part answer to this question. I've spoken long enough, and now I'd like for you all to respond with your thoughts. What do you think?" Professor Johnson asked the class. A student at the front of the class opened the comments.

"Well, we started with the myth of African inferiority. I think that one of the greatest threats to the ego of Europeans was the discovery of the Egyptian civilization. For so much history, intellectualism, and works of art to be credited to African people probably seemed ludicrous to them, so they found ways to either claim these great things for themselves or separate Egypt from the rest of Africa like a different people inhabited it altogether."

"I agree," another student chimed in. "And after that, the inferiority myth was perpetuated to justify slavery, 100%. If Africans and Negroes were deemed subhuman, closer to the 'beasts of the field,' then slavery could be hailed a good thing, a saving grace, so to speak. Morally, slave owners would feel justified before God and fellow men."

A third student remarked, "Today, there is no doubt that whites benefit from the system of racism in our country. Myths about black inferiority sustain that racism, where criminal justice and mass incarceration can profit private prisons, mass entertainment featuring dangerous black criminals or even no black cast members at all can make millions for executive producers, and the beauty industry can profit from foreign hair."

"Wow!" Professor Johnson replied. "What excellent remarks. I agree with you all on this. The effect of the myth of black inferiority is indeed wide and deep. There is no doubt that whites have and continue to benefit from this narrative, although motivations may have slightly changed over time. With such a prolonged history, I wonder what the future benefit will be for whites who continue to perpetuate this myth. One thing is certain, and that is that more and more people, particularly African Americans, are becoming aware of these tactics and myths, and they are seeking to both expose and overturn them. Let's take another break and reconvene in 10 minutes."

After the break, Professor Johnson returned to his PowerPoint to display a political propaganda piece from a 1900 North Carolina election. The drawing depicted a heathenishly caricatured black man with a devilish body and haunting, black face. The man had a long, winding tail, pointed wings that read "NEGRO" on the left wing and "RULE" on the right, and in the grasp of his claws and sharp nails were frightened white people. White women were attempting to flee from him. The black man stood on a box that read "Fusion Ballot Box" and he was surrounded by complete blackness and haunted-looking trees.[36]

Myth #3: The Black Man is Violent and Prone to Hyper-Criminality

"Now, there is one last concept that I want to address in today's

[36] "Negro Rule" North Carolina elections. (n.d.). Retrieved from Reddit: https://www.reddit.com/r/PropagandaPosters/comments/2jfir5/negro_rule_north_carolina_elections_1900/

class, and that is the myth that the black man is violent and prone to hyper-criminality. This image of the black savage and brute, who is prone to violent thinking and behavior, who enjoys bloodshed, and who is seeking to destroy his white counterpart is most recognizable and most worrisome today, yet it has existed for centuries. We will, similar to the last myth, dissect this concept from the point of view of the colonized African, the Negro slave, and the modern African American."

Professor Johnson then began his lecture. "Within the journals of many Europeans colonizers, missionaries, and invaders were descriptions of Africans as violent savages. They were placed amidst a dangerous, foreign, and testy landscape, a continent filled with dense jungles, savanna, and undiscovered civilizations. Among them were large, wild creatures like lions, rhinos, crocodiles, elephants and gorillas. Their weaponry primitively consisted of spears and shields. And sometimes, they were depicted as cannibals.

"Wendy Hamlet, author of *Savage Constructions: The Myth of African Savagery*, writes, 'In the glory centuries of the various European empires, modern 'civilized' nations launched a vast assault upon small kinship groups of generally self-sufficient peoples around the globe...European colonials named Africans 'savages' to justify their treatment of the (for the most part) peaceful generous peoples that welcomed them into their villages. Europeans savaged the people of Africa, but justified their savagery by naming Africans savages.'[37]

---

[37] Hamblet, W. (2009, November 12). 'Civilisation' and the myth of African 'savagery'. Retrieved from Pambazuka News: http://www.pambazuka.org/governance/%E2%80%98civilisation%E2%80%99-and-myth-african-%E2%80%98savagery%E2%80%99

"Colonialists in the West took great advantage of this myth to solidify and cement the system of slavery. What better way to tame and restrain the Negro labor force than by fear tactics which aimed to keep white masters on guard and in suspicion of insurrection? Throughout the antebellum South, stories of radicalized, defiant, and dangerous Negro slaves began to emerge and spread. A great fear of rebellion, like Nat Turner's in 1831, caused masters to always be on guard and propelled them to enforce strict rules and punishment on the plantation.[38]

"It wasn't until Reconstruction from 1867-1877 that overt portrayals and images of the violent black man began to emerge. Without the controlling hand of slavery, many whites feared that Blacks would return to their animalistic instincts and seek retaliation. As a result, a devastating and ugly 'black peril' emerged. During this time, scientific racism called for eugenics and insisted upon the violent and hypersexual racial instincts of Blacks.

"Between 1882 and 1951, a dramatic increase in lynchings occurred (4,730 according to Tuskegee Institute data) for both actual and perceived crimes.[39] The Jim Crow era resulted in the abuse and deaths of many Blacks. This was justified because of white fear, particularly the fear of Blacks overtaking white women who were deemed the prized

---

[38] Hamblet, W. (2009, November 12). 'Civilisation' and the myth of African 'savagery'. Retrieved from Pambazuka News: http://www.pambazuka.org/governance/%E2%80%98civilisation%E2%80%99-and-myth-african-%E2%80%98savagery%E2%80%99

[39] Caricatures of African Americans: The Brute. (2012, November 25). Retrieved from Authentic History Center: http://www.authentichistory.com/diversity/african/4-brute/

possessions of the South. I firmly believe that this era was the one in which the stereotypes of the African Americans as hyper-criminal and hypersexual really began to stick in America. We have yet to fully shake them.

"Today, the stereotype of the 'black thug' abounds. It is perpetuated through media and entertainment on a daily basis; while at the same time, statistics on crime and incarceration are touted by politicians and officials as 'proof' that this stereotype must be true.

"Let's consider the media first. Media injustice in America has abounded since slavery, and today it rears its head on TV, in movies, and in music through images of the black gang member, hustler, pimp, drug dealer, or convict. If I were to ask you, right now, to write a list of every movie or TV show that you've seen depicting African Americans in such a way, we would be here for the remainder of the day. We consume these images almost from birth, and you can imagine the effect they have on the self-esteem and collective conscious of African American men.

"Even the mainstream news, a system that declares itself 'objective' and 'unbiased,' consistently perpetuates stereotypes through framing, labels, and misinformation. Consider the 1994 *Time* cover featuring a darkened and shadowed O.J. Simpson with the phrase 'An American Tragedy' beneath him in large, red letters. In New York's Audubon Ballroom in 1964, Malcolm X said, 'This is the press, an irresponsible press. It will make the criminal look like he's the victim and make the victim look like he's the criminal. If you aren't careful, the newspapers will have you hating the people who are being oppressed and loving the people who are doing the oppressing.'[40] And yet, media irresponsibility has contributed to the creation of real and impacting social attitudes, as the Opportunity Project demonstrated in its 2011 *Social Science Literature Review*.[41] In it, they explored causal links between media and public attitudes, including:

- General antagonism toward black males
- Exaggerated views, expectations of, and tolerance for race-based socio-economic disparities
- Exaggerated views related to criminality and violence
- Lack of identification with or sympathy for black males
- Reduced attention to structural and other big-picture factors
- Public support for punitive approaches to problems

"Furthermore, the tendency for people to mistake the media world for the real world, especially when they do not have exposure to or experience with African Americans in the real world (e.g., like in many rural areas around the country) contributes to a detrimental mindset about African Americans. These views have real-world implications which are hard to ignore, like harsher sentencing by judges, lower job prospects, and increased chances of deadly interactions with the police.[42]

[40] Savali, K. (2015, June 2). Throw Away the Script: How Media Bias Is Killing Black America. Retrieved from The Root:
http://www.theroot.com/articles/culture/2015/06/how_media_bias_is_killing_black_america/
[41] Social Science Literature Review: Media Representations and Impact on the Lives of Black Men and Boys. (2011, October). Retrieved from The Opportunity Agenda:
http://www.racialequitytools.org/resourcefiles/Media-Impact- onLives-of-Black-Men-and-Boys-OppAgenda.pdf
[42] Social Science Literature Review: Media Representations and Impact on the Lives of Black Men and Boys. (2011, October). Retrieved from The Opportunity Agenda:

"Scientifically, the hyper-criminality of African Americans is argued through statistics on crime and incarceration which traditionally do not consider correlative factors such as poverty, mental illness, social injustice, and education. In the era of the Black Lives Matter movement, high rates of 'black on black' crime are routinely cited by conservatives as methods of diverting crucial conversations on deadly policing along with racial disparities in the criminal justice system. Numbers are cited, often incorrectly, to imply that African Americans engage in a disproportionately high amount of crime and violence.

"Noticeably, rates of white on white crime are conveniently left out of the discussions. The truth is that rates of black on black homicide (90% according to U.S. Department of Justice in 2015) are in fact much closer to the rate of white on white homicide (82% according to the same source) than most are willing to acknowledge.[43]

"In a November 2015 article, "Policing 2016", Samuel Bieler and Jesse Jannetta from the Urban Institute, write, 'When socioeconomic differences are controlled for, the case for black hyper-criminality gets even weaker. Despite the research, violence in black communities is frequently brought up to derail policy conversations about the justice system and its effect on black

http://www.racialequitytools.org/resourcefiles/Media-Impact- onLives-of-Black-Men-and-Boys-OppAgenda.pdf

[43] U.S. Department of Justice. (2014). Expanded Homicide Date Table 6. Retrieved from FBI:UCR: https://ucr.fbi.gov/crime-in-the-u.s/2014/crime-in-the-u.s.-2014/tables/expanded-homicide-data/expanded_homicide_data_table_6_murder_race_and_sex_of_vicitm_by_race_and_sex_of_offender_2014.xls

communities."[44] Furthermore, they assert that when white-on-white violence is either misreported or left unsaid, it implies that African Americans are uniquely violent.

"What's most dangerous about tactics like these is that they are being used to influence attitudes today, which, in turn, affect who people vote for to represent them in office. Many of our candidates for office are successfully running on platforms of 'Law and Order' and 'Stop and Frisk' and gaining wild support because of these misconceptions and stereotypes. Without champions of truth, including students like you, the majority of Americans are being led to continue to believe myths about negative racial instincts.

"Let's remember that Blacks make up roughly 13% of the U.S. population while whites make up 64%. Now, here are some truths about black criminality which must be considered when we talk about the problem of black violence in America:[45]

- Blacks are more likely to be arrested for committing the same crimes as whites
- Blacks are convicted more often than whites for committing the same crime
- Blacks are more likely to be sentenced to jail than whites convicted of the same crime

[44] Bieler, S. (2015, November 24). Elevating the 2016 Debate: Crime and Justice; What the data really say about race and homicide. Retrieved from Urban Institute: http://www.urban.org/2016-analysis/what-data-really-say-about-race-and- homicide

[45] Farbota, K. (2016, September 2). Black Crime Rates: What Happens When Numbers Aren't Neutral. Retrieved from The Huffington Post: http://www.huffingtonpost.com/kim-farbota/black-crime-rates-your- st_b_8078586.html

- 100 white people and 74 black people might be arrested
- 50 white people and 48 black people might be convicted
- 19 white people and 24 black people might be sentenced to prison

"There are some undeniable systemic differences in how Blacks and whites are treated by the law. That does not mean that Blacks are more prone to violence than whites; it means they are being arrested, convicted, and sentenced at higher rates than whites for committing the same crimes. You, right here, and the people around you embody and experience the truth about African Americans. African Americans have proven to live peaceably since slavery. They've even protested peaceably. The number of peaceful and productive organizations, movements, churches and causes which have been birthed in the face of systemic racism and discrimination is remarkable. The myth of the violent black man is just that—a myth."

At the end of the class, Professor Johnson announced that the next class would be devoted to poverty. He asked the students to come prepared to discuss the following: poverty and related concepts, statistical highlights, the impact of poverty on African American communities, families and diverse populations. We will also discuss the way we were (yesterday), the way we are (today), and the way we need to be (tomorrow). After giving them the assignment, he dismissed the class.

PART IV
Poverty

Poverty

There is something about poverty that smells like death. Dead dreams dropping off the heart like leaves in a dry season and rotting around the feet; impulses smothered too long in the fetid air of underground caves. The soul lives in sickly air. People can be slaveships in shoes.

Zora Neale Hurston

To be a poor man is hard, but to be a poor race in a land of dollars is the very bottom of hardships.

W.E.B. DuBois, *The Souls of Black Folk*

Professor Johnson was prepared to answer questions from one or two curious students following the miseducation class, but he did not anticipate the multitude of emails in his inbox when he checked it the following day. The students had a ton of questions about Professor Johnson's lecture, and they wanted to know where they could find more information about the topic. There were even a couple of messages from new students who, after hearing about the class from their friends, were interested in taking the course next semester. Naturally, he invited them to attend the next class on poverty for a "drop-in" session.

Of all the buzz and excitement that was generated from the day, Professor Johnson was most grateful for his nieces' and nephew's attention and responses. According to Grandma Johnson, they could not stop talking about their family tree, and how they hoped to one day know the African countries where their ancestors were born. Professor Johnson was thrilled; he was curious about the questions that Keith and Sandra might have for their teachers the next day in school, and he silently prayed that they would be able to answer them appropriately. If not, he thought, he would eventually hear about it later and answer them himself.

The night before the class on poverty, Aunt Mildred advised Uncle John to only allow Keith and Sandra to attend the class.

"Little Jeannie might be too young to understand everything you're going to cover," she said. "Let her stay here with me, and we will watch some relevant kid's shows about the matter. I want her to understand that she should be grateful for what she has, and that a lot of people are less fortunate than she is. Keith and Sandra will be able to follow along with your students, dear," she finished. Uncle John agreed, and on the evening of his class, he stopped by Grandma Johnson's to pick up the older kids. For this class, he asked them to be his helpers by controlling the PowerPoint clicker and passing out the handouts he prepared. They eagerly agreed and assumed their positions as soon as they arrived to the classroom. The students filed in unusually early this afternoon, and as expected, there were a couple of new faces among the crowd.

Professor Johnson welcomed everyone and asked the drop-ins to introduce themselves. He was glad to hear that an economics major and a criminal justice major were present among the visitors, and he thought they might have some interesting points to add during the class discussion.

At 3:00 p.m. sharp, Professor Johnson began class. He started with a Frederick Douglass quote from his 1886 speech in Washington, D.C. on the 24th Anniversary of Emancipation which said: "Where justice is denied, where poverty is enforced, where ignorance prevails, and where any one class is made to feel that society is an organized conspiracy to oppress, rob, and degrade them, neither persons nor property will be safe."

"This is a class on poverty," Professor Johnson stated. "But, like the other discussions in this series, we will look at poverty from a unique perspective. Today, I want to examine poverty in the African American community and from an historical and analytical perspective. This discussion will be in keeping with the themes from our last class on miseducation. In addition to looking at current trends and data, I want us to explore some root issues and systems which have made poverty what it looks like today in the black community. In no way will I suggest that poverty and its effects are exclusively felt by the black community. The majority of people living in poverty in the United States (U.S.) are white, and we are going to dig into actual numbers later on. The reason that I am going to single out the black experience, in this class, is that it contributes to our overall understanding of the unique and often tragic experience of a community whose history is like no other in modern history.

"If you remember, when we first started this series, I explained the analogy of the Three Blind Mice. I said that the blindness experienced by each mouse represents an inhibiting ailment imposed on the African American community. They are mental illness, miseducation, and poverty. Of all three, I believe that poverty is the most complex and complicated blindness, incredibly immune to simple solutions or antidotes, because it produces so many other debilitating circumstances. Poverty fuels mental illness, miseducation, crime, substance abuse, poor eating habits, and family breakdowns unlike any other system. We can call these things side effects of the blindness.

"Furthermore, I believe that these conditions are felt by the African American community in a way that is slightly different from any other race or community in the world. Hear me now: I did not say that the African American community has it worst when it comes to poverty; that is not true when we consider global poverty. What I am saying is that African American poverty was formed differently, and at times purposefully, as a result of the system of American slavery. And, we will explore this history today.

"As usual, I am a bit ahead of myself. Last class, I assigned some research to you and I'm sure you have found a lot of relevant and interesting material. Along with your research, here is what we are going to cover today:

- The definition and foundational understanding of poverty

- African Americans' first exposure to poverty

- The development of poverty in the African American community from emancipation onward

- Current poverty rates and the face of poverty today

- Poverty's impact on the African American family and the community

As always, I value your input and knowledge. I will open the class for a shared discussion intermittently, and I encourage you to take notes. You might even begin to think of some answers to the problems that we're facing here. Write them down and please share them with me after class."

The Definition of Poverty

Professor Johnson nodded to Keith to dim the lights and begin the PowerPoint.

"Let's start with the definition of poverty," Professor Johnson began. "I'm going to give a simple version, and together, we will construct an expanded one. Merriam-Webster defines poverty as 'the state of being poor; a lack of something; the state of one who lacks a usual or socially acceptable amount of money or material possessions.'[46]

"Poverty looks different throughout the world, and there is no

---

[46] Definition of Poverty. (n.d.). Retrieved from Merriam-Webster: http://www.merriam-webster.com/dictionary/poverty

clear-cut definition or measure for it across the board. While definitions of poverty are varied, there is one that I particularly like, and it is described by the World Bank Organization this way."

Professor Johnson nodded again to Keith, and Keith moved to the next slide, which read:

> *Poverty is hunger. Poverty is lack of shelter. Poverty is being sick and not being able to see a doctor. Poverty is not having access to school and not knowing how to read. Poverty is not having a job, is fear for the future, living one day at a time.*[47]

"The way that poverty is measured in the United States has come under some scrutiny for being too simplistic and one-dimensional. The World Bank reports that there are multiple dimensions of poverty which have many indicators that currently are not measured. Based on your research at home, can anyone explain to us how poverty is measured in the United States?"

"I can," a student responded. "Here's the simple version: If a household earns less (per year) than the amount determined by the U.S. Census Bureau for its size, then they are considered to be below the poverty level. Here's a more complex explanation: Every year, the U.S. Census Bureau estimates the level of income needed to meet basic needs, and that is calculated by 'tripling the inflation-adjusted cost of a minimum food diet in 1963 and adjusting for family size, composition and the age of the householder.'[48]

[47] What is poverty? (n.d.). Retrieved from Economic and Social Inclusion Corporation: http://www2.gnb.ca/content/gnb/en/departments/esic/overview/conten t/what_is_poverty.html
[48] How is poverty measured in the United States? (2016, September 13). Retrieved from Center for Poverty Research: http://poverty.ucdavis.edu/faq/how- poverty-measured-united-states

"This is called the poverty threshold. Those households who earn less than the threshold are considered to be in poverty. The Bureau estimates annual poverty rates by surveying about 95,000 sample households across the country. The sample excludes those who are homeless and not in shelters, single military personnel who live alone, and people living in institutions.

In addition, The Bureau indicates four comparative classifications related to the poverty threshold: 'above the poverty level' for household incomes above 100% of the threshold; 'near poverty' for households above 100% but below 125% of the threshold; 'in poverty' for households at or below 100% of the threshold; and 'severe' or 'deep poverty' for households below 50% of the threshold. In 2015, the poverty threshold for a family of four, including two adults and two children, was $24,036."[49]

"I have something to add here," another student chimed in. "In my research, I found that there are differences between the poverty threshold, which is issued by the Census Bureau for statistical purposes, and poverty guidelines, which are issued by the Department of Health and Human Services for the determining of financial eligibility for certain programs like food stamps. For instance, the poverty guideline in 2015 for a family of four was $24,250; that's $214 more than the threshold.[50] I didn't realize the difference before I researched it."

"Thank you for that comprehensive explanation," Professor

[49] How is poverty measured in the United States? (2016, September 13). Retrieved from Center for Poverty Research: http://poverty.ucdavis.edu/faq/how- poverty-measured-united-states
[50] 2015 Poverty Guidelines. (2015, September 3). Retrieved from U.S. Department of Health & Human Services: https://aspe.hhs.gov/2015- poverty-guidelines

Johnson responded. "Those guidelines are extremely important because they determine eligibility for necessary programs like free or reduced lunch for kids at school, free health care, or nutrition assistance. The analytics of it all can become a bit technical, as our classmates just demonstrated, but those analytics have some real and powerful effects on the way that many people experience life in the United States."

"As we expand our definition of poverty," a third student added, "I'd like to share a small excerpt from a powerful letter that I found online called 'What is Poverty?' by Jo Goodwin Parker. It was published, with Mrs. Parker's permission, in a 1971 book by George Henderson titled *America's Other Children: Public Schools Outside Suburbs*.[51] Take a listen:

> Poverty is being tired. I have always been tired. They told me at the hospital when the last baby came that I had chronic anemia caused from poor diet, a bad case of worms, and that I needed a corrective operation. I listened politely— the poor are always polite. The poor always listen. They don't say that there is no money for iron pills, or better food, or worm medicine. The idea of an operation is frightening and costs so much that, if I had dared, I would have laughed. Who takes care of my children? Recovery from an operation takes a long time. I have three children. When I left them with "Granny" the last time I had a job, I came home to find the baby covered with fly specks, and a diaper that had not been changed since I left. When the dried diaper came off, bits of my baby's flesh came with it. My other child was playing with a sharp bit of broken glass, and my oldest was playing alone at the edge of a lake. I made

[51] Parker, J. (n.d.). "What is Poverty?". Retrieved from Michigan State University: https://msu.edu/~jdowell/135/JGParker.html

twenty-two dollars a week, and a good nursery school costs twenty dollars a week for three children. I quit my job. Poverty is dirt. You can say in your clean clothes coming from your clean house, "Anybody can be clean." Let me explain about housekeeping with no money. For breakfast, I give my children grits with no oleo or cornbread without eggs and oleo. This does not use up many dishes. What dishes there are, I wash in cold water and with no soap. Even the cheapest soap has to be saved for the baby's diapers. Look at my hands, so cracked and red. Once I saved for two months to buy a jar of Vaseline for my hands and the baby's diaper rash. When I had saved enough, I went to buy it and the price had gone up two cents. The baby and I suffered on. I have to decide every day if I can bear to put my cracked sore hands into the cold water and strong soap. But you ask, why not hot water? Fuel costs money. If you have a wood fire it costs money. If you burn electricity, it costs money. Hot water is a luxury. I do not have luxuries. I know you will be surprised when I tell you how young I am. I look so much older. My back has been bent over the wash tubs every day for so long, I cannot remember when I ever did anything else. Every night I wash every stitch my school age child has on and just hope her clothes will be dry by morning..."

"This is DEEP POVERTY," Professor Johnson remarked to a stunned and silent class. "It is clear that the experience of poverty looks and feels a lot different from the way that it is simply defined on paper. It makes me wonder whether those of us who are comfortably removed from it can truly understand the urgency of fixing it, including our policymakers and administrators. I wonder how many of us personally know a woman like Mrs. Parker. I imagine that it can be difficult to champion for a cause that we are not personally familiar with.

"We don't know this for sure, but let's imagine that Mrs. Parker is African American. How much wider would the gap become between our policymakers' experiences and her reality? These are some of things that we must think about as we examine poverty in the context of the Three Blind Mice.

"Now, at the time that Mrs. Parker's story was shared, 1971, 37.1% of African American families with children headed by single mothers were living in poverty.[52] That's over 1/3 of African American households in Mrs. Parker's time. The overall poverty rate in the U.S. at that time was 12.5%. So, how did we get here? Let's move to a discussion on the development of poverty in the African American community. This is going to look and sound a lot like a history lesson, but it's an integral part of the story of how we got to where we are today."

African Americans' First Exposure to Poverty

Professor Johnson waved to Sandra to pass the first handout to the class. She did so eagerly. Each student received a copy of a comprehensive timeline that Professor Johnson prepared.

"If you look at the timeline that Sandra has just passed out, you will notice that I start with slavery", Professor Johnson noted, from the moment that the first enslaved African arrived here in 1619 on the White Lion, a Dutch ship, and was traded to the colonialists as an indentured servant, poverty existed in the black

---

[52] Edelman, P. (2012, June 22). The State of Poverty in America. Retrieved from The American Prospect: http://prospect.org/article/state-poverty-america

community.[53] Poverty is not a measurable form like the U.S. Census Bureau analyzes today, but a poverty like the one Mrs. Parker describes, and one that was faced by most of the early colonists of that time.

"A dire need for laborers fueled indentured servitude in America as the colonies expanded and as settlers flooded in from 1618 to 1623. While many Africans worked under contract as indentured servants in exchange for shelter and food, they experienced a gradual change to chattel slaves, and by 1654, John Casor became the first legal slave in America.[54] From the 1650's onward, the slave code developed, which defined the slave narrative that we are familiar with today.

"There is no doubt that poverty in the 1600s, 1700s and 1800s looked a lot different than it does today. A lot of early settlers were barely getting by as a result of disease, malnutrition, and conflicts with Native Americans. Yet, colonies expanded with advancements in agriculture, tobacco, sugar and cotton became high-demand exports from the South; and large-scale plantations were established. Slave labor became a cemented institution in the American South to support all of this. The small, wealthy, white elite rose to prominence—on the backs of that same labor.

"Slaves relied almost completely on their masters for their basic needs—food, water and shelter—and did not legally own or possess anything, including themselves. This is a poverty which cannot be

[53] History of Slavery in America. (n.d.). Retrieved from Open Computing Facility, Berkeley University: https://www.ocf.berke ey.edu/~arihuang/academic/abg/slavery/history.ht ml
[54] History of Slavery in America. (n.d.). Retrieved from Open Computing Facility, Berkeley University: https://www.ocf.berke ey.edu/~arihuang/academic/abg/slavery/history.ht ml

compared or measured based on our current notion of the term, which considers access to food as one of its primary indicators. Slaves were generally denied access to healthy food, proper health care, appropriate social activities, or family structure. These standards of 'poor' and 'not poor' were beginning to be defined for the first time in our country—and they were characterized by access.

"In the Antebellum South, we see the first large-scale unequal distribution of wealth in the country's history. This proved to be the launching pad through which economic and social inequality gaps widened between whites and African Americans, resulting in a more recognizable poverty which many African Americans have inherited to this day. In a 2014 *Boston Globe* article, "Where slavery thrived, inequality rules today," correspondent Stephen Mihm explains it this way:[55]

> In 2002, two economic historians, Stanley Engerman and Kenneth Sokoloff, published an influential paper that tried to answer a vexing question: why are some countries in the Americas defined by far more extreme and enduring levels of inequality—and by extension, limited social mobility and economic underdevelopment—than others?
>
> The answer, they argued, lay in the earliest history of each country's settlement. The political and social institutions put in place then tended to perpetuate the status quo. They concluded that societies that began 'with extreme inequality

[55] Mihm, S. (2014, August 24). Where slavery thrived, inequality rules today. Retrieved from Boston Globe: https://www.bostonglobe.com/ideas/2014/08/23/where-slavery-thrived- inequality-rules-today/iF5zgFsXncPoYmYCMMs67J/story.html

tended to adopt institutions that served to advantage members of the elite and hamper social mobility.' This, they asserted, resulted in economic underdevelopment over the long run.

"We cannot separate the problem of poverty in the African American community today from slavery and the many inequalities that it produced. The two, as Mihm alludes, are closely intertwined. This is the reason why I part ways with anyone who suggests that because slavery is over, that everything is fair and balanced for African Americans in this country, or, that because we've had a black president, that equality is promised to all. This could not be farther from the truth, and today we are seeing reality play out in front of us in communities throughout America.

"Now, let's move to emancipation and beyond. What did African American economics looks like once Blacks were legally free and had to be paid for their labor? Many thought that the economic playing field became equal upon emancipation. Mihm explains, 'The destruction of slavery did not destroy all the political institutions, social mores, and cultural traditions that sustained it. Nor did it make public institutions, of the kind that the north had been building for decades, suddenly come into being.'[56] Let's look at post-slavery history to examine why.

---

[56] Mihm, S. (2014, August 24). Where slavery thrived, inequality rules today. Retrieved from Boston Globe: https://www.bostonglobe.com/ideas/2014/08/23/where-slavery-thrived- inequality-rules-today/iF5zgFsXncPoYmYCMMs67J/story.html

Development of Poverty from Emancipation Onward
Reconstruction: 1865-1877

"Reconstruction marked the transformative period following the American Civil War during which the South faced social, economic and political rebuilding. Years earlier, Lincoln's Emancipation Proclamation, his 'military necessity' to preserve the Union, caused an unexpected turn in the War by declaring all slaves free by January 1, 1863. Blacks showed up by the thousands to enlist in the Union Army, and it became clear that a social revolution was unavoidable whether the South won the war or not. Lincoln's strategy proved effective; however, the War was over by early 1865.[57]

"On December 18, 1865, the Thirteenth Amendment was ratified and slavery was officially abolished. President Andrew Johnson's (1865-1869) presidential reconstruction was underway and the landscape began to change dramatically in the South. Blacks, although free, faced extreme hostility from financially devastated and morally crushed whites. Although Johnson's reconstruction efforts were lenient (he only required that southern governments uphold the 13th Amendment, swear loyalty to the Union and pay off their war debts), this did not prevent the southern states from taking a protective and emboldened stance against real progress for negroes.[58]

"Despite the South's backlash against reconstruction, later

---

[57] Reconstruction. (n.d.). Retrieved from History.com: http://www.history.com/topics/american-civil-war/reconstruction
[58] Reconstruction. (n.d.). Retrieved from History.com: http://www.history.com/topics/american-civil-war/reconstruction

culminating in the Hayes-Tilden Compromise of 1877, Blacks experienced unprecedented, yet unfruitful, economic and social autonomy. The Freedmen's Bureau worked to distribute land confiscated by the Union Army to give to former slaves in 1865, but the efforts were eventually thwarted by Johnson's decision to revert them; however, the Bureau would fight to assist refugees and freed slaves in the coming years.[59]

"The resulting relationship that began to form between Blacks and whites during this time is astoundingly recognizable today. Many whites, faced with the reality that Blacks no longer had to do certain work, began to label black workers as lazy, entitled and undisciplined. I'd like to note here, because it is both interesting and telling, that attitudes toward the perceived entitled haven't changed much. The *LA Times*, for instance, just published an article titled, "How do Americans view poverty?" 'Many blue-collar whites, key to Trump's presidency, criticize poor people as lazy and content to stay on welfare.'[60] I encourage you to read the article in your spare time and note the parallels between then and now. During reconstruction, many contractual disputes were brought by whites against 'indolent' black workers which had to be mediated by the Freedmen's Bureau. Whites' desire and quest to secure a submissive and satisfied labor force was met with fierce opposition. Blacks, faced with the resentment of years of slavery and harsh conditions, now had options, even though limited.

---

[59] Reconstruction, America's First Attempt to Integrate. (n.d.). Retrieved from African American Registry: http://www.aaregistry.org/historic_events/view/reconstruction-americas- first-attempt-integrate

[60] Lauter, D. (2016, August 14). How do Americans view poverty? Many blue-collar whites, key to Trump, criticize poor people as lazy and content to stay on welfare.
Retrieved from LA Times: http://www.latimes.com/projects/la-na-pol- poverty-poll/

"At the same time, new labor systems emerged to replace slavery (e.g., sharecropping and wage labor), and few freedmen became landowners overnight. The sharecropping system involved workers keeping one-third to one-half of the crops on rented land for themselves with the rest going to the landowners, a system that promoted poverty and dependence as cotton prices began to fall and sharecroppers began owing more to their landowners than they were able to repay. Furthermore, many African Americans were forced, under threat of violence, to sign exploitative sharecropping contracts which promoted the system of poverty within the community.[61]

"Many southern whites themselves, without slave capital and facing losses from Confederate bonds, also faced poverty following the War. They were forced to borrow money to resume farming, falling into debt and having to grow cotton themselves. Both black and white farmers began falling into a cycle of debt which had crippling effects.[62] Many men took on tiring manual labor while many women worked as domestic servants. Most Blacks were excluded from working in the tobacco and textile factories that white workers flocked to, which impeded their ability to gain income. In the northern cities, Blacks encountered wider employment opportunities.

"On another note, the topic of voting and labor rights for Blacks had become prevalent just prior to Lincoln's assassination, yet many southerners vehemently disapproved of black suffrage and

[61] Sharecropping. (n.d.). Retrieved from History.com: http://www.history.com/topics/black-history/sharecropping
[62] From Slave Labor to Free Labor. (2003). Retrieved from Digital History: http://www.digitalhistory.uh.edu/exhibits/reconstruction/section3/section 3_intro.html

land ownership. What was Johnson's position, you ask? The federal government had no right to determine state's legislation. As a result, states took matters into their own hands, banding together through 'patriotic' groups like the Ku Klux Klan and enacting 'Black Codes' to restrict Blacks' activity and force their hands to almost pre-Civil War labor arrangements.[63] Whatever gains were made during reconstruction were soon thwarted by fierce opposition in the South.

Post-Reconstruction: 1875-1900

"This was made possible when the Hayes-Tilden Compromise of 1877 forced U.S. troops to pull out of the South (specifically, Louisiana, South Carolina, and Florida), formally ending the reconstruction era. The swift, informal deal was made following a contested election and resulted in Republican Rutherford Hayes being awarded the White House over Democrat Samuel Tilden. Without military oversight and Republican backing, the states were free to exercise 'home rule,' resulting in a wide loss of African American rights.[64] Ironically, the deal and several private meetings preceding it took place at the Wormley Hotel, which was owned and operated by a prominent free black man named James Wormley. His hotel was internationally renowned and catered to prominent businessmen and politicians—the Washington elite. For this reason, the Hayes-Tilden Compromise

---

[63] Reconstruction, America's First Attempt to Integrate. (n.d.). Retrieved from African American Registry: http://www.aaregistry.org/historic_events/view/reconstruction-americas- first-attempt-integrate

[64] Reconstruction, America's First Attempt to Integrate. (n.d.). Retrieved from African American Registry: http://www.aaregistry.org/historic_events/view/reconstruction-americas- first-attempt-integrate

is often called the 'Wormley Compromise.'[65]

"Following the Compromise and the end of reconstruction, many whites simply could not fathom a world where Blacks walked and worked and voted and learned just like whites. They did everything they could to prevent that from becoming a reality, and words like 'home rule' became prevalent. The codes were repressive, and they promoted segregation and disenfranchisement at astounding levels.

During this time, the first black exodus took place, with African Americans spreading and concentrating in northern cities such as New York, Philadelphia, Pittsburgh, Cleveland and Chicago by 1890.[66] Many were fleeing poverty and racial violence in the South. Similarly, the 'exoduster' movement saw more than 40,000 Blacks settle in Kansas (where they purchased over 20,000 acres of land in the 1880s), Oklahoma, and Colorado.[67] For the first time, predominantly black communities began to emerge, like the community of Nicodemus in Kansas. Many arrived impoverished, sick, and desperate. Combined with white resentment, some of these communities did not last long.

"We can imagine the plight of many Blacks during reconstruction and immediately following when promises of equality and civil rights began to fade with white rage, racism and the reality of poverty. Blacks were more educated, more literate, electable to

[65] Graves, D. (n.d.). Wormley Hotel. Retrieved from The White House Historical Association: https://www.whitehousehistory.org/wormley-hotel- 1
[66] Reconstruction and Its Aftermath. (n.d.). Retrieved from African American Odyssey: https://memory.loc.gov/ammem/aaohtml/exhibit/aopart5.html
[67] Exodusters: Black Migration to Kansas after Reconstruction. (n.d.). Retrieved from Geni: https://www.geni.com/projects/Exodusters-Black-Migration-to- Kansas-after-Reconstruction/9276

local offices, and socially autonomous for the first time in American history. The church became the social, political and economic hub of the black community, and it also initiated charitable movements to support those in need.[68] Yet Blacks worked relentlessly to fight institutionalized racism and discrimination in the same communities.

"The post-reconstruction era was the Jim Crow era, and the fight for civil rights was conducted in the courtroom. Although discrimination in public places was prohibited by the Civil Rights Act of 1875, the Supreme Court overturned the Act in 1883, describing those as social rights and not civil rights which were to be guaranteed by the states. Soon, southern states enacted laws that legalized racial segregation, culminating in the landmark *Plessy v. Ferguson* case which set forth the separate but equal doctrine. Well, we all know that segregated facilities were rarely equal, and the money trails proved that to be so.[69] In the South, more money was spent on white schools than on black schools, for instance. Let's stop here for a moment and open this up for a quick discussion: Why does it matter that more money was spent on white schools than black schools, and what does it have to do with poverty?"

A student answered, "Lack of education is one of the driving forces of poverty. Many African Americans were already less educated than whites coming out of slavery, and the schools that the states offered for them, especially in the South, were inferior. This probably rang true for other public services in those

---

[68] Reconstruction and Its Aftermath. (n.d.). Retrieved from African American Odyssey: https://memory.loc.gov/ammem/aaohtml/exhibit/aopart5.html
[69] African-Americans after Reconstruction. (n.d.). Retrieved from Cliffs Notes: https://www.cliffsnotes.com/study-guides/history/us-history-ii/american- society-and-culture-18651900/africanamericans-after-reconstruction

communities, like public libraries. I read somewhere yesterday that in 1857, 393 public libraries existed in Pennsylvania, whereas only 26 existed in South Carolina.[70] This systematically set the stage for some of the disparities that we see today between 'white' schools and 'urban' schools, where resources are often disproportionately assigned. And, research has shown a close link between poverty and a lack of education."

"Very good point," Professor Johnson responded. "Despite the tragic events of this era, we cannot forget the achievements and legacy of prominent black scholars, educators and artists during this period. Some call this era, from the 1870s to the start of World War I, the 'Booker T. Washington Era.' Institutions of higher learning awarded more degrees to Blacks than ever before, and many rose to prominence by receiving their doctorates. W.E.B. DuBois and Carter G. Woodson received their doctorates from Harvard University. Black training schools and colleges like the Tuskegee Institute provided agricultural and vocational training and access to higher learning. Voices like Washington and DuBois represented diverse black perspectives, with Washington adopting a more compromising approach to segregation while DuBois supported diligence in protest and voting.

"In addition, the National Association for the Advancement of Colored People (NAACP) and the National Urban League (NUL) were founded during this time. This progress, combined with the astounding creative gains that were made by black artists and performers like Paul Laurence Dunbar and the Fisk Jubilee

---

[70] Mihm, S. (2014, August 24). Where slavery thrived, inequality rules today. Retrieved from Boston Globe: https://www.bostonglobe.com/ideas/2014/08/23/where-slavery-thrived- inequality-rules-today/iF5zgFsXncPoYmYCMMs67J/story.html

Singers are a testament to the overcoming and diligent spirit of Blacks.[71] Financial, educational and social success stories abounded for many African Americans, but they were not the reality for the majority of Blacks of the time."

The Great Depression: 1929-1939

"World War I provided an opportunity for Blacks to unite in protest against racism at home and abroad. Black soldiers fought heroically and often underappreciated in segregated support units. The NAACP worked case by case to dismantle legal segregation while black artists and activists fought for intellectual and creative recognition through movements like the Harlem Renaissance. Not long after the war, the Great Depression caused mass suffering throughout the country.

"Considering the post-reconstructionist conditions discussed earlier, it's no surprise that Blacks were in an economically depressed state long before the stock market crash of 1929. About 150,000 Blacks fled Georgia in the 1920s to escape the agricultural crisis as cotton prices plummeted. By 1933, for instance, cotton prices dropped from eighteen cents per pound to less than six cents per pound, affecting some 12,000 black sharecroppers.[72] Many throughout the South migrated, occupying urban centers and seeking city jobs in the North and Midwest. During the Depression, unemployment rates rose to an estimated 31.7 percent among whites, and among Blacks, the 'last hired and first fired,'

---

[71] The Booker T. Washington Era. (n.d.). Retrieved from African American Odyssey: https://memory.loc.gov/ammem/aaohtml/exhibit/aopart6.html

[72] African Americans, Impact of the Great Depression on. (n.d.). Retrieved from GALE, U.S. History: http://ic.galegroup.com

the unemployment rate was over 50%.[73] Popular slogans of the time included, 'No Jobs for Niggers Until White Man Has a Job,' and 'Niggers, back to the cotton fields, city jobs are for white folks.' Violence was common and encouraged by whites to create job vacancies while a Depression-era 'slave market' forced Blacks to work for only dollars per week and at 30% below the rates of white workers.

"Roosevelt's New Deal promised equity and resources for Blacks, which some received through programs like the Works Progress Administration (WPA) and New Deal writing projects. However, Roosevelt was criticized for not being fervent enough in protecting Blacks from discrimination and segregation at the state level and in implementation of New Deal policies. Blacks were often shorted of social services and benefits provided to whites, especially in the agricultural arena. The New Deal was quickly referred to as the 'raw deal' by many Blacks and would continue to be until the mid-30s when they began to receive broader access to programs.[74]

"By 1939, New Deal work and relief programs were considered a 'godsend' by Blacks who were benefitting from the programs and occupying about one-third of housing projects. Advancements were fueled by the increase of organized labor unions and political activism by Blacks. Communities responded to economic and social plights through networking and community-based alliances. Blacks shared resources from childcare to washing machines, often

---

[73] The Great Depression. (n.d.). Retrieved from Amistad Digital Resource: http://www.amistadresource.org/plantation_to_ghetto/the_great_depressi on.html
[74] African Americans, Impact of the Great Depression on. (n.d.). Retrieved from GALE, U.S. History: http://ic.galegroup.com

supporting one another, while churches launched their own welfare programs. Black attorneys and intellectuals fought for greater economic equality in the courtroom while social and economic activists unionized to ensure fair labor practices at work. The NAACP, NUL, the Communist Party, and other organizations worked diligently to bring attention to the economic plight of blacks, publicize the inequalities of the New Deal programs, and achieve minimum wages and hours.[75]

"These coalitions achieved many socio-economic successes between 1935 and 1939, but racial discrimination was still persistent. By the late 30s and on the brink of WWII, many whites had returned to full-time employment while Blacks remained dependent on social welfare and relief programs.

World War Two: 1939-1945

"Where the New Deal could not fully reinvigorate the nation's economy, World War II did. Following the outbreak of the war, black families migrated north to fill shortages in manufacturing which provided high wages, new job skills, and greater economic opportunities than those provided in the South by an agrarian economy. As the war progressed, more than 700,000 black families moved North, fleeing Jim Crow segregation in the South and occupying urban centers which ironically resulted in increased racial tensions in the cities.[76]

[75] Sustar, L. (2012, June 28). Blacks and the Great Depression. Retrieved from SocialistWorker.org: http://socialistworker.org/2012/06/28/blacks-and- the-great-depression
[76] Hodges, K. (n.d.). Continuity or Change: African Americans in World War II. Retrieved from UMBC: http://www.umbc.edu/che/tahlessons/pdf/Continuity_or_Change_Africa n_Americans_in_World_War_II(PrinterFriendly).pdf

"Blacks were determined not to fight or work under the same discriminatory conditions as in the previous war, and many hoped to find equality of opportunity in the military. In the realm of government defense contracting, for instance, only 240 out of 10,000 aircraft worker positions were offered to African Americans in 1940. Under threat of protest in the form of a March on Washington (MOW) organized by Civil Rights leader A. Philip Randolph, Roosevelt issued Executive Order 8802, which banned discrimination in government hiring and established the Fair Employment Practice Committee (FEPC) to investigate reports of non-compliance.[77]

"This did not stop Blacks from being alienated to support roles such as cook, quartermaster and grave digging duties while working for the government. Black journalists responded with the 'Double V Campaign' heralded by the black newspaper, *The Pittsburgh Courier*, which promoted a mission for Blacks to unite to gain victories abroad and at home. Over 2.5 million blacks registered for the draft during WWII and over one million served. Blacks around the country faced questions like, 'Should I sacrifice my life to live half American? Is the kind of America I know worth defending?' These questions and others were posed in a letter to the editor of the *Courier*, published on January 31, 1942, with an overwhelmingly enthusiastic response from its readers.[78]

"During the war, many black heroes emerged, like Mess Attendant

[77]Hodges, K. (n.d.). Continuity or Change: African Americans in World War II. Retrieved from UMBC: http://www.umbc.edu/che/tahlessons/pdf/Continuity_or_Change_Africa n_Americans_in_World_War_II(PrinterFriendly).pdf

[78] Jr., H. L. (n.d.). What Was Black America's Double War? Retrieved from WHRO: http://www.pbs.org/wnet/african-americans-many-rivers-to- cross/history/what-was-black-americas-double-war/

Doris 'Dorie' Miller, who aided his shipmates and captain aboard the *U.S.S. West Virginia* at Pearl Harbor. He was the first black sailor to receive the Navy Cross. The Tuskegee airmen were trained on a segregated base as part of the Army Air Force and became legendary for their heroism and decorations. Black women served through the Women's Auxiliary Army Corps (WAAC) and in nursing units, although they did so in segregation as well.[79]

"At home, the Double V campaign became extremely popular, promoted through pop culture and mainstream events. Celebrity and political endorsements followed, and they ran weekly in the *Pittsburg Courier* until 1943. By fall of 1945, the Double V insignia was removed from the paper and was replaced by a single V in 1946. In 1948, the campaign realized one of its main goals: President Harry Truman signed Executive Order 9981, which ordered the desegregation of the U.S. armed forces.[80] Many credit the work done by the campaign and civil rights leaders during WWII for laying the groundwork for the civil rights protests of the 1950s and 1960s.

"I believe that World War II marked the beginning of a shift in the economic conditions of African Americans, Professor Johnson continued. Abigail and Stephan Thernstrom summarize the shift in their 1998 article, "Black Progress: How far we've come, and how far we have to go:"[81]

---

[79] African Americans in World War II: Fighting for a Double Victory. (n.d.). Retrieved from National WWII Museum: http://www.nationalww2museum.org/assets/pdfs/african-americans-in-world.pdf
[80] Taylor, C. (n.d.). Patriotism Crosses the Color Line: African Americans in World War II. Retrieved from The Gilder Lehrman Institute of American History: https://www.gilderlehrman.org/history-by-era/world-war-ii/essays/patriotism-crosses-color-line-african-americans-world-war-ii
[81] Thernstrom, A. a. (1998, March 1). Black Progress; How far we've come, and how far we have to go. Retrieved from Brookings: https://www.brookings.edu/articles/black-progress-how-far-weve-come-and-how-far-we-have-to-go/

'Thus by 1960 only one out of seven black men still labored on the land, and almost a quarter were in white-collar or skilled manual occupations. Another 24 percent had semi-skilled factory jobs that meant membership in the stable working class, while the proportion of black women working as servants had been cut in half. Even those who did not move up into higher-ranking jobs were doing much better.

A decade later, the gains were even more striking. From 1940 to 1970, black men cut the income gap by about a third, and by 1970 they were earning (on average) roughly 60 percent of what white men took in. The advancement of black women was even more impressive. Black life expectancy went up dramatically, as did black homeownership rates. Black college enrollment also rose—by 1970 to about 10 percent of the total, three times the pre-war figure.'

Postwar to Today

"The postwar period also marked a huge shift in the way that our country talked about, defined, measured and addressed poverty, Professor Johnson added. Relatively speaking, the scientific and social study of poverty only began towards the end of the nineteenth century and focused on white poverty.[82] Interest in poverty naturally peaked at the height of the Great Depression,

---

[82] Gilens, M. (2003). How the Poor Became Black: The Racialization of American Poverty in the Mass Media. Retrieved from The University of Michigan: https://www.press.umich.edu/pdf/9780472068319-ch4.pdf

waned as the war caused the American economy to grow, and was 'rediscovered' in the 1960s by the public and by policymakers like John F. Kennedy, who was particularly moved by the poverty he saw in West Virginia.[83] The poverty threshold, and official data on the matter, date back to 1963, after economist Mollie Orshansky developed the metric."[84]

"I read about Kennedy's attention to the impoverished regions of the country and some of his anti-poverty programs of the early 1960s", a curious student noted. "They included education and training programs and federal assistance. He is purported to have been inspired by Michael Harrington's *The Other America*, a 1962 exposé which dispelled the notion that poverty was not an issue in America and revealed the 'invisible land' of the poor which was over forty million strong.[85] With Harrington, Daniel Patrick Moynihan and Office of Economic Opportunity Chief Sargent Shriver as consultants, President Kennedy and then President Johnson began to formulate an anti-poverty agenda to address this problem."

"Ah, yes. You're referring to the War on Poverty," Professor Johnson replied. "What many don't know is that when poverty first became a social issue up until this time, the dominant image of poverty was 'the white rural poor of the Appalachian

[83] Gilens, M. (2003). How the Poor Became Black: The Racialization of American Poverty in the Mass Media. Retrieved from The University of Michigan: https://www.press.umich.edu/pdf/9780472068319-ch4.pdf

[84] Fisher, G. (1992). The Development and History of the Poverty Thresholds. Retrieved from Social Security Bulletin: https://www.ssa.gov/history/fisheronpoverty.html

[85] Isserman, M. (2012). 50 Years Later: Poverty and The Other America. Retrieved from Dissent Magazine: https://www.dissentmagazine.org/article/50- years-later-poverty-and-the-other-america

coalfields,'[86] not Blacks. This was propagated through mass media coverage, which portrayed poor people as predominantly white up until about 1964. Consider, for example, Mark Pilisuk's book, *Poor Americans: How the White Poor Live*. Very few people noticed or talked about black poverty, and you will not find many resources on the topic before the 1960s."

"That is strange to think about when you consider the amount of media and academic attention that is paid to the topic of black poverty today," the same student noted.

"Indeed," Professor Johnson said. "In 1965, there seemed to be a decided shift in the way that the media, particularly news magazines, characterized the poor. Let's take a closer look at the War on Poverty, the Civil Rights Movement, and the black racialization of poverty, which seemed to go hand-in-hand during this time.

"Where Kennedy's administration introduced the need for anti-poverty programs in the early 1960s, Johnson turned it into a full-fledged agenda by 1964. In his State of the Union address that year, he declared 'an unconditional war on poverty,' and went on to say:

> Very often a lack of jobs and money is not the cause of poverty, but the symptom. The cause may lie deeper in our failure to give our fellow citizens a fair chance to develop their own capacities, in a lack of education and training, in

---

[86] Gilens, M. (2003). How the Poor Became Black: The Racialization of American Poverty in the Mass Media. Retrieved from The University of Michigan: https://www.press.umich.edu/pdf/9780472068319-ch4.pdf

a lack of medical care and housing, in a lack of decent communities in which to live and bring up their children.

But whatever the cause, our joint Federal-local effort must pursue poverty, pursue it wherever it exists--in city slums and small towns, in sharecropper shacks or in migrant worker camps, on Indian Reservations, among whites as well as Negroes, among the young as well as the aged, in the boom towns and in the depressed areas.[87]

"That same year, Johnson passed the Economic Opportunity Act (EOA) of 1964, which set in motion a number of initiatives including: the Job Corps, the Volunteers in Service to America (VISTA) program, a federal work-study program, and several others. The Office of Economic Opportunity (OEO), responsible for implementing these new initiatives, was also formed through EOA. Johnson also passed the Food Stamp Act of 1964, which was proceeded by the pilot program.

"The following year, the Social Security Amendment of 1965 was ratified, creating Medicare and Medicaid and expanding Social Security benefits for retirees, widows, the disabled, and college-aged students. Finally, the Elementary and Secondary Education Act of 1965 established the Title I program providing subsidies for schools with large populations of impoverished students.[88]

---

[87] Johnson, L. B. (1964, January 8). Annual Message to the Congress on the State of the Union. Retrieved from The American Presidency Project: http://www.presidency.ucsb.edu/ws/?pid=26787
[88] Matthews, D. (2014, January 8). Everything you need to know about the war on poverty. Retrieved from Washington Post: https://www.washingtonpost.com/news/wonk/wp/2014/01/08/everything-you-need-to-know-about-the-war-on-poverty/

"You can bet that many of these initiatives would not have been passed without the fervent support and pressure of the Civil Rights Movement. A concerted fight for legal and social equality years prior to the War on Poverty culminated in the passage of the Civil Rights Act of 1964 and the Voting Rights Act of 1965. Coming off the heels of a memorable decade of passionate and organized activism in the form of boycotts, sit-ins, demonstrations, protests and marches, activists now turned their full attention towards economic inequality. The NAACP, the NUL, and others partnered with the Johnson Administration to see that the EOA was passed.

"This is where we begin to see the real shift in attention towards black poverty in America. Activists like Dr. Martin Luther King, Jr. worked to bring attention to the plight of poor Blacks living in northern urban centers, initiating the Chicago Freedom Movement and the 1968 Poor People's March on Washington. Intense collective behavior in the summer of 1964 lead to riots in Harlem, Rochester, Chicago, Philadelphia and New Jersey. With the dramatic and forced shift of attention to the black ghettos, racial tensions became incredibly high. This seemed to culminate in the Watts Riot of 1965, in which the Los Angeles neighborhood saw a six-day riot that resulted in 34 deaths (31 of them Black), 900 injured, and 4,000 arrests.[89] Further riots in 1966 and 1967 occurred throughout the country.

"Would you be surprised, then, if I told you that in news magazine coverage of poverty (specifically from *Time*, *Newsweek*

---

[89] Gilens, M. (2003). How the Poor Became Black: The Racialization of American Poverty in the Mass Media. Retrieved from The University of Michigan: https://www.press.umich.edu/pdf/9780472068319-ch4.pdf

and *U.S. News and World Report*), the proportion of African Americans in pictures of the poor was 27% in 1964, while in 1967, that proportion rose to 72%? African Americans have dominated media images of the poor since then.[90] Mind you, this has been occurring as white middle class has been eroding, and vast income gaps between it and the upper class of whites has formed.

"The rise of the image of 'black poverty' ironically coincided with a fall in support for the OEO and anti-poverty efforts. For one, President Johnson needed increased congressional support for America's participation in Vietnam, something that Dr. King lamented when he noted that the War on Poverty was being 'shot down on the battlefields of Vietnam.'[91] Consequently, the anti-poverty initiatives never saw the funding necessary to fully implement its programs. Following Johnson's presidency, Nixon largely dismantled the OEO and spread its functions to an array of other federal agencies. The office was closed for good in 1981, yet many of the anti-poverty programs created by the War on Poverty exist to this day, including Medicaid, Medicare, food stamps, Head Start, Job Corps, VISTA and Title I."[92]

A student in the back asked, "Was the War on Poverty effective or not?"

---

[90] Gilens, M. (2003). How the Poor Became Black: The Racialization of American Poverty in the Mass Media. Retrieved from The University of Michigan: https://www.press.umich.edu/pcf/9780472068319-ch4.pdf

[91] Bauman, R. (n.d.). War on Poverty. Retrieved from Blackpast.org: http://www.blackpast.org/aah/war-poverty

[92] Matthews, D. (2014, January 8). Everything you need to know about the war on poverty. Retrieved from Washington Post: https://www.washingtonpost.com/news/wonk/wp/2014/01/08/everythi ng-you-need-to-know-about-the-war-on-poverty/

"Good question," Professor Johnson replied. "Did anyone do research on this particular topic?"

"Sure, I did," a student said in the front. "The answer is yes, and no, depending on who you ask. In 2012, economists at Columbia University examined poverty before and after the government's involvement in the form of taxes and transfers. What they found was poverty decreased from 26% in 1967 to 16% in 2012.[93] So it is clear that the anti-poverty programs did have some lasting effects when you factor in the number of people who literally rise above the poverty threshold, also, when Supplemental Nutrition Assistance Program (SNAP) benefits, housing subsidies, social security and tax credits are taken into account. Those benefits are not counted as sources of income when determining poverty levels.

"Proponents of the War on Poverty also point to its success in democratizing America through the establishment of community programs, particularly those in the black community, which exist to this day. These programs, inspired by the activism demonstrated during the civil rights and black power movements, provided jobs, training, housing, credit unions and cultural programs.[94]

"On the other hand, conservatives and others claim that the War on Poverty did nothing but create an economy in which too

[93] Matthews, D. (2014, January 8). Everything you need to know about the war on poverty. Retrieved from Washington Post: https://www.washingtonpost.com/news/wonk/wp/2014/01/08/everythi ng-you-need-to-know-about-the-war-on-poverty/
[94] Bauman, R. (n.d.). War on Poverty. Retrieved from Blackpast.org: http://www.blackpast.org/aah/war-poverty

many people became, and continue to be, dependent on welfare. From 1964 to 2012, U.S. taxpayers spent trillions of dollars on anti-poverty programs, and progress against poverty in its traditional measure has been minimal. That is because, as I just mentioned, the government does not factor in income from benefits in its measure of poverty rates. In so doing, the welfare system has continued to expand in cost. In this regard, it is considered a failure, because it did not produce Johnson's intended outcome of increasing self-sufficiency."

"That is an excellent explanation," Professor Johnson remarked. "And it brings us to our final two points of discussion for today: current poverty rates and the impact of poverty on the African American community today. Sandra is passing out a sheet which lists some basic statistics on poverty for the most recent year that we have data, 2015.

Poverty Rates[95]

Overall Poverty Rate: 13.5% (43.1 million people)

Percent of people who fell below the poverty line—$24,250 for a family of four—in 2015

Twice the Poverty Level: 31.7% (100.9 million people)

Percent of people who fell below twice the poverty line—$48,500 for a family of four—in 2015

Half the Poverty Level: 6.1% (19.4 million people)

Percent of people who fell below half the poverty line—$12,125 for a family of four—in 2015

---

[95] Basic Statistics. (n.d.). Retrieved from Talk Poverty: https://talkpoverty.org/basics/

Child Poverty Rate: 19.7% (14.5 million people)

Percent of children under age 18 who fell below the poverty line in 2015

African American Poverty Rate: 24.1% (10.0 million people)

Percentage of African Americans who fell below the poverty line in 2015

Hispanic Poverty Rate: 21.4% (12.1 million people)

Percentage of Hispanics who fell below the poverty line in 2015

White Poverty Rate: 9.1% (17.8 million people)

Percentage of non-Hispanic Whites who fell below the poverty line in 2015

"The facts are clear. The black poverty rate is higher than the rate of any other ethnicity in the United States. This has been the case for many years. The poverty rates for African American households headed by a single parent are even more alarming. This second handout demonstrates, in chart form, the history of black poverty from 1967 to 2014:[96]

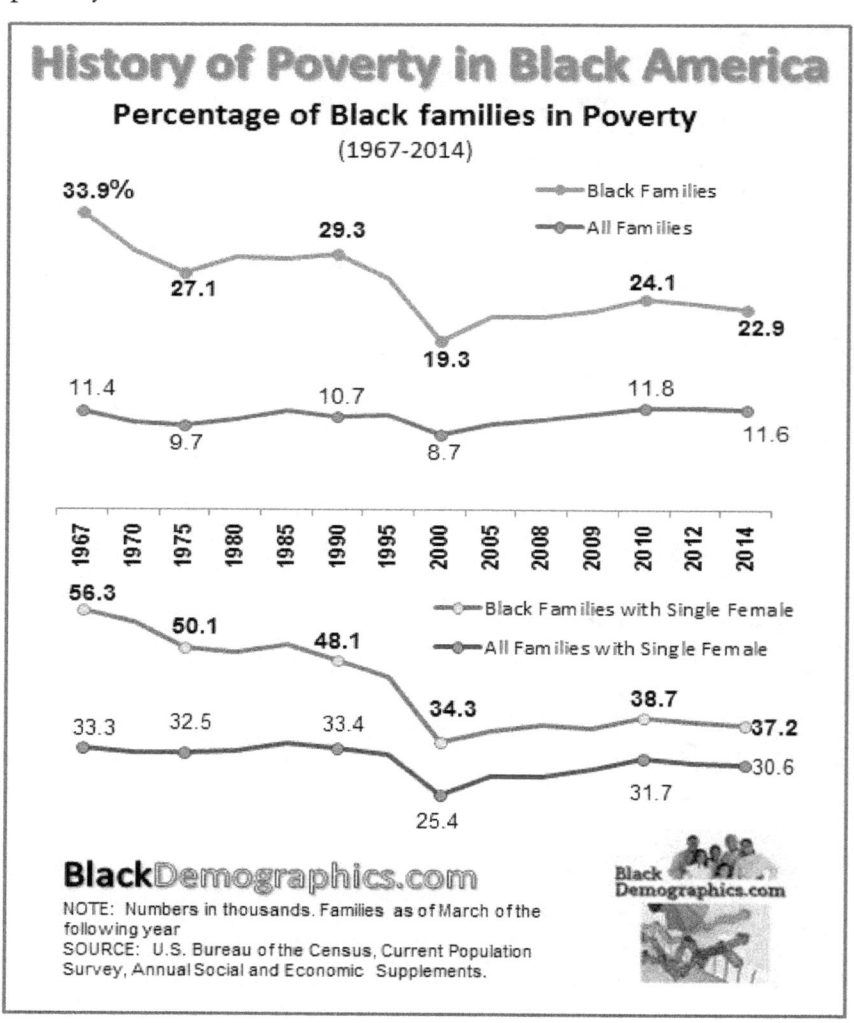

History of Poverty in Black America

Percentage of Black families in Poverty
(1967-2014)

Black Families
All Families

33.9%
29.3
27.1
24.1
22.9
19.3
11.4
10.7
11.8
9.7
8.7
11.6

1967 1970 1975 1980 1985 1990 1995 2000 2005 2008 2009 2010 2012 2014

Black Families with Single Female
All Families with Single Female

56.3
50.1
48.1
34.3
38.7
33.3   32.5   33.4
37.2
25.4
31.7
30.6

BlackDemographics.com

NOTE: Numbers in thousands. Families as of March of the following year
SOURCE: U.S. Bureau of the Census, Current Population Survey, Annual Social and Economic Supplements.

Black Demographics.com

[96] http://blackdemographics.com/households/poverty/

"Those are the facts, now here is the explanation to the question: 'What does poverty in the African American community look like today?' Today, black poverty looks a lot like:

- Undesirable, poorly maintained housing in dense, segregated communities

- Neighborhoods with a high concentration of families living in poverty; most are poor

- Single-parent families with children, with the provider working one or more minimum wage jobs

- Limited high-end groceries and markets, which means limited access to healthy and fresh foods

- Fewer medical resources in close distance (e.g., doctors offices, dental offices)

- Crowded schools, understaffed schools with high drop-out rates and high discipline rates

- Neighborhoods with a high police presence with a lot of arrests and charges for minor offenses

"Poverty is indeed a relative issue, and it does not look the same in each country. Poverty in America is as complex as the racial, societal and institutional factors which characterize and influence it. For Blacks in poverty, it affects everything from education to job prospects to family structure, and we need to understand its history in order to fully address it. My hope is that we started to tackle some of this in today's class. We can combine what you've learned in our previous classes, and what we cover today to begin to help charter a course forward to alleviate these problems. Thank you."

The presentation on poverty was the last class. Professor Johnson was pleased with his students' performance throughout the semester. They demonstrated mastery of curriculum content; they were committed and focused. Projects were thoroughly researched, information was detail-oriented and innovatively presented. When four of the students asked Professor Johnson if they could become involved in some of his community-based initiatives, he was delighted. He asked them if they would be interested in helping him plan, develop and implement the Mayor's Family Empowerment and Community Development Summit. They were excited and jumped at the opportunity. Professor Johnson could not be more pleased.

During dinner and their "chillax" time, Mildred asked John about plans for the Family Empowerment and Community Development Summit. She also showed him an article in the evening paper, *The Newark Pilot*, which explained that the summit is a part of the City's Change the Community Initiative (CCI). The press release said, in part, that community change begins with changing mindsets and habits of the people within the community and those who provide services to them.

Mildred said, "John isn't that a powerful image of where we are today?"

"Yes dear," John said. "I postulate that change begins with illumination."

PART V
Illumination

"Wisdom is the principal thing; therefore get wisdom;
and with all thy getting get understanding."

Proverbs 4:7

Illumination: The Family Empowerment and Community Development Summit

Professor Johnson's students diligently began to conduct background research, contact and consult with subject matter experts, and develop marketing plans. The professor was preparing to meet with the mayor's handpicked City-wide Advisory Committee for Community Development (CACCD). The CACCD consists of representatives from government agencies, educational institutions, faith-based communities and health fields—to name a few. The CACCD is interdisciplinary, experienced and devoted. Professor Johnson's students are some of the brightest and best; therefore, they spent time on tasks and worked harmoniously. They titled the summit "Illumination: Prescriptions to Help Build Stronger Families and Better Communities."

The CACCD presented a list of scholars, researchers, mental health practitioners, educators, government officials and authors who accepted the mayor's invitation to participate in the Family Empowerment and Community Development Summit (Summit). The website and flyer for marketing were also presented and approved. The CACCD agreed on the focus of the Summit: Enlightenment, Information and Tools, Transformation, Collaborative and Cooperative Partnerships, and Solutions to Current and Emerging Problems. Thereafter, they all participated in an exciting marketing campaign to reach families and agencies throughout the city—and that they did! Flyers, radio announcements and public relation media blitzes were everywhere!

Family Empowerment and Community Development Summit

ILLUMINATION: Prescriptions to Help Build Stronger Families and Better Communities

The Family Empowerment and Community Development Summit is designed to help build community capacity, relationships and services to enrich the lives of residents and make neighborhood stronger.

Our Focus:

- Enlightenment
- Information and tools
- Transformation
- Collaborative and cooperative partnerships
- Solutions to past, current, and emerging problems

Come out and participate in learning sessions and workshops conducted by subject matter experts, hear keynote speeches and panel discussions, obtain valuable resources and much more!

Where	Dates	Time
Newark Civic Arena North Main Street Newark, NJ	June 21-23, 2017	Friday: 6pm Saturday: 8:30am - 4:30pm Sunday: 9am - 2pm

150

After three months of meticulous planning and registrations which exceeded expectations by 50%, the Summit began. It started on Friday evening and lasted throughout Sunday afternoon.

FRIDAY EVENING: A Model for Family Empowerment and Community Development

Douglas Washington, the Mayor of Newark, opened the Summit with a welcome address. He explained the goals of Illumination, how it fits with the Change Community Initiative (CCI), the city's strategic plan and projected outcomes. He acknowledged all of the invited guests and thanked the community and those who worked behind the scenes. He also acknowledged and thanked representatives from Washington, D.C., the President's executive departments: Agriculture, Commerce, Defense, Education, Energy, Health and Human Services, Homeland Security, Housing and Urban Development, Interior, Labor, State, Transportation, Treasury, and Veterans Affairs, as well as the Attorney General. The group was making tours and site visits of selected cities to make policy and program recommendations to the legislative branch. The mayor was proud that his city was chosen and that the timing was great—they could report his work in progress. After the mayor's welcome, Professor Johnson moderated the Summit.

He previewed the agenda, introduced the speakers, workshop facilitators and all of the presenters. The opening general session was devoted to community development which was in keeping with the much talked about theme: "It takes a village to raise a child", and a much needed "cradle to grave paradigm." The speaker for the session was Dr. Carolyn Wilson, Director of Housing and Urban Development's (HUD) Office of Community Planning and Development. Her office is responsible for helping cities form partnerships among all levels of government and private sectors, including for profit and non-profit organizations to provide decent housing, suitable living environments and expand economic opportunities for low and moderate income persons.

Her session was an excellent opening because community development requires collaborative and cooperative relationships with all of the components of the service delivery system. She first gave a general definition of community relating to shared values and roles in social institutions such as family, home, work and society and explained that community development is a process where community members come together to take collective action and generate solutions to common problems. She paused to congratulate the mayor and the architects of the Summit for focusing on family empowerment as a part of the CCI because the life and viability of a community is predicated, in part, on the mindset of the people (i.e., the families who live there and the people who provide services to them).

She boldly proclaimed, "It's time to go back to some of the policies and programs that were geared to needs of urban communities, look at what worked, what didn't, and strategically go forth with plans for change." She projected and explained a reality-based model, which she developed to get the audience to think about, revisit and buy into a comprehensive community development paradigm.

A Six Step Model for Family Empowerment and Community Development

Step 6	Implement	
Step 5	Revise Step 2 (Produce New Paradigms)	
Step 4	Strengths, Weaknesses, Opportunities, and Threats	
Step 3	Monitoring Services and Programs	
Step 2	Policies, Resources and Program Development	
Step 1	Citizen Participation	

"The interesting thing about this model," she said, "is that it is a blend of an old concept and a much needed new one. For example, The Poverty Bill, also known as the Economic Opportunity Act, was passed in 1964 and established such federal programs as Head Start, Volunteers in Service to America (VISTA), Upward Bound, Talent Search and Student Support Services (TRIO), and Job Corps. President Lyndon Johnson, who introduced the War on Poverty legislation, believed in expanding the federal government's role in education and health care as reduction strategies. In 1965, The Food Stamp Act, Elementary and Secondary Education Act and Social Security Acts were passed. A major requirement for the planning and development of the programs, which grew out of the War on Poverty initiatives, was citizen participation. Citizen participation gave communities opportunities to express their needs, provided a basis for shared values, trust and identity. The exchange of ideas and information contributed to and produced inclusion to as opposed to the exclusion from prevalent social, political and economic decisions.

"Grassroots people are not involved in planning and developing programs and services that they need. It is for that reason that I included a citizen participation component in my model to influence policies and program development, monitoring all efforts, a report of findings, a Strengths, Weaknesses, Opportunities and Threats (SWOT) analysis and going back to the drawing board. We needs to work on the needs of families and empower them to move from where they are: whether on welfare, working to take care of the household because of an absent father or one who is in jail or prison, babies having babies, drug addiction, and gang involvement. We need to start improving homes and the lives of family members and then move out of homes to the community where we are supposed to serve and meet articulated needs."

Dr. Wilson's presentation was powerful and she received a thunderous applause and standing ovation. Before she left the podium, she told the audience that she was available throughout the entire Summit and welcomed an opportunity to further discuss any comments and concerns that they wished to share. The first evening of the Summit ended with an invitation for the audience to visit with the team of coaches and mentors who were there to provide consultation and technical assistance.

Professor Johnson projected the agenda for the next day. It consisted of a series of workshops, lectures, a panel discussion and some video highlights.

SATURDAY- It Takes a Village

"Good morning everyone! I hope you enjoyed our close out session with our coaches and mentors. Let's give them a hand clap of our thanks," said Professor Johnson. "And how about breakfast? Shout out to the restaurant staff! Let's get right into our full agenda for today. Our focus is family. Then we will move to our 'It Takes a Village' segment where we talk about community services or a service delivery system—what we have and what we need."

He continued, "Our speaker this morning is Dr. Calvin Randolph. He is internationally known as a 'double hitter' because he is a physician and clinical psychologist; he wears the two hats well. His bio is in your Summit package, so I will not share his impressive credentials and numerous honors at the moment. I'll just say, congratulations for all that you have done and do, not just for African Americans, but for your global contributions. We are proud and honored to have you today. Let's give him some love as he comes to us now!"

The audience rose to their feet and clapped loudly and continuously until he thanked them and asked them to take their seats.

The Family

"Good morning and thank you for inviting me to your Summit. I am, indeed, honored to be here. I am humble and most grateful. I must congratulate your mayor for this Summit, and moreso, for his CCI. It is a much needed undertaking, long overdue throughout the USA, and we need to do all that we can to help bring about change.

"This morning, I want to talk about the family. The family is the smallest unit of a society and, therefore, critical to its development and maintenance. When I talk about family, I think first about two great scholars and authors: Dr. Andrew Billingsley and Dr. Robert Hill and their outstanding works, which provide valuable insights. In Billingsley's book, *Black Families in White America*, he analyzed the history, problems and aspirations of the black family in a society that is controlled by white people. He posited that the goal of the black family is to break free of white institutions and that they must manage their own institutions before they can make maximum contributions to their own community and the larger community. Managing their own institutions, from my perspective, can mean managing one's home and family.

"It should be noted that Billingsley also pointed out that black families have shown an amazing ability to survive in the face of brutalities, hardships and insurmountable conditions. Surviving, as we have historically done, requires strength. In *The Strength of Black Families*, Dr. Robert Hill identified five family strengths, which for Blacks constitute adaptations necessary for survival and to get ahead in a hostile, white controlled environment. The five strengths, essential strengths, are: (1) strong kinship bonds; (2) a strong work orientation; (3) adaptability of family roles, a response to economic necessities on the part of black, low-income families; (4) high achievement orientation; and (5) religious orientation.

"Dr. Hill and Dr. Billingsley assert that understanding strengths as well as weaknesses can lead to developing proper programs to help meet the multi-faceted and multifarious needs of African Americans today.

"The problems menacing African American families are well-known and well-documented, so I don't have to speak on them. Moreover, the Urban League's *Annual State of Black America* publication does an outstanding job, which I encourage you to get a copy and read. You can download it for free online. For now, I want you to visualize this picture:

Mary is a 25-year-old mother with diabetes and five children; two of the children are in elementary school (first and second grade) and the other two are dropped off at their grandmother's five to six days a week. She lives in the inner city in public housing. She has two "baby daddies"— one is in prison and the other one is strung out on drugs. She works in housekeeping at a motel across town earning minimum wage. She has to catch two buses every day, one to take the children to her mother's and another bus to get to work. Mary's paycheck cannot take care of the bare necessities— food, clothes, and shelter, plus miscellaneous expenses that always emerge.

"Poor Mary, what did she do, and what can others do to help her?"

Dr. Randolph ended his talk by making a transition to the next speaker. He said, "Our next speaker, Dr. Joseph Nixon, is my colleague and friend. He is Director of Health and Human Services, Baltimore, MD where he just won the Governor's award for Community Service Excellence. Let's welcome him as he comes to tell us what Mary did and how we can help her."

Dr. Nixon began his presentation without the usual fanfare. He simply said, "Good Morning. I am here to tell you about Mary. You just heard her profile, but little did you know that Mary can be used to explain a community's service delivery system. But, let me first answer the question that the previous speaker left you with: What did Mary do about her situation? Mary became depressed; she started drinking, missing days from work, neglecting her children and eventually had a nervous breakdown. He asked, What can we do to help her, or better still, what can the community do?"

"Help for Mary," he continued, "is based on some internal factors and external factors. First, from an internal perspective, it is important to consider **what's within Mary**: her philosophy of life, her self-esteem, personal values, family values, parenting ability and things that are important to her. A person's thoughts and heart often influence their behavior. Also, consider **what's in Mary's house**: the man (or men), the relationships she has with them; the relationship that the men and other people have with her children, and how she manages resources and runs the house."

"Know this," Dr. Nixon said with vehemence, "just like it takes a village to raise a child, it takes a village to save some parents and adults! I call that village a community and I posit that the community has some services and resources that Mary and so many others like her need. Illumination is about getting people to understand problems and giving them tools and resources to help resolve them. With Mary, I see some things, can't you?
Sure you do. When you see something, you must do something! So let's talk about solutions.

"I ask our stellar guests and experts on: social services, education and recreation, housing, banking and finance, criminal justice and corrections, health services and transportation to join me on stage. Audience, please give them a hearty applause as they come."

The clapping sounded like thunder, but it ended once everyone was seated. Dr. Nixon told the audience that he had a series of questions for the Summit guests to answer in the form of panel discussions.

> **Question 1**: What can social service agencies (Health, Education, Housing and Labor) do to help low income families?

> **Question 2**: How can community agencies provide support to help female heads of households?

> **Question 3**: What can be done to improve the criminal justice system?

> **Question 4**: What are other problems and concerns that need to be addressed?"

Four panels discussed Dr. Nixon's questions and related ones from the audience. Professor Johnson's students captured the responses and made an impressive PowerPoint called ILLUMINATION:

QUESTION 1

What can social service agencies (Health, Education, Housing, Labor, and Recreation) do to help low income families?

HEALTH

Some of the major problems are: diabetes, cardiovascular disease, HIV/AIDS, cancer, mental illness, and gun violence

Some of the solutions include: Regular medical and psychological check-ups, screenings such as mammograms, colonoscopies, chest x-rays, and blood work, proper nutrition, exercise, medication, education, and personal and community empowerment

EDUCATION

Some of the major problems are: Inadequate funding for schools, school violence, drop-out rates, student achievement gaps, and lack of adequate and equitable resources

Some of the solutions include: Community control of schools, curricula tailored to meet student needs and job requirements, counseling, mental health programs, community-based teachers, tutorial programs, adequately prepared teachers, cooperative parent-teacher relationships

HOUSING

Some of the major problems are: Housing discrimination, depressed neighborhoods, financial resources, and ecological systems (trust and control)

Some of the solutions include: Housing assistance programs, fair housing policies, safe neighborhoods, and opportunities for home ownership

LABOR

Some of the major problems are: Poverty, employment discrimination, chronic unemployment, underemployment, lack of skills for jobs in high growth industries, minimum wage, lack of opportunities for youth, business ownership, and restrictive banking.

Some of the solutions include: Job development, training for jobs in key industries (e.g.; manufacturing, engineering, and industrial maintenance), increasing minimum wage, financial remedies for victims of discrimination, enforcing non-discrimination obligations for federal contracts and subcontracts, salary equity for men and women, entrepreneurship training and assistance, and black-owned banks.

QUESTION 2

How can community agencies provide support to help low income female heads of households?

ILLUMINATION

ILLUMINATION

SINGLE-
FEMALE

Some of the major problems are: Staying emotionally and physically healthy, affordable and reliable childcare, coping with children's' behavioral problems, financial problems, distress, depression, jail or incarceration of the man of the house, personal congruence and incongruence, and spiritual disconnectedness.

Some of the solutions include: Self-help organizations, day-care facilities, after-school programs, subsidized and informal childcare arrangements, parenting classes, distress and anger management, employability development training, and finding support and using it. Private, non-profit and government agencies should develop special programs to meet their mental, physical, and spiritual needs.

ILLUMINATION

ILLUMINATION

COMMUNITY

Some of the major problems are: Lack of empowerment, lack of leadership and leadership development, need for community control, and citizen participation.

Some of the solutions include: Leadership development, membership participation (community engagement), strengthen cohesion, strategic and tactical planning, implementation, and political involvement.

163

Q U E S T I O N   3

What can be done to improve the criminal justice system?

ILLUMINATION

ILLUMINATION

Some of the major problems are: Prevention, the adjudication process, and the imprisonment process.

Some of the solutions include: Start with community policing. At least 60% of the police need to live in the communities that they are policing. There needs to be decentralized prosecution. More African American judges are needed; they must also live in the community. The prisons and jails should provide adequate opportunities for education, job training and mental health services. Conjugal visitations are needed. Spiritual development is suggested. Prisons need to be located where the majority of the prison population reside. Drug treatment programs are needed for addicted prisoners.

QUESTION 4

What other problems and concerns need to be addressed?

Mental Illness Concerns and Recommendations

I. Trauma

TRAUMA is an extremely stressful event that overwhelms a person's psychological and physiological ability to cope. It results in extreme fear and helplessness. Trauma includes responses to such incidents as accidents, natural disasters, deaths, childhood sexual abuse and violence.

Recommendations:

- Professional counseling and psychotherapy
- Talk to empathetic listeners
- Mobilize and or join an existing support system
- Challenging exercises
- Relaxation exercises
- Well-balanced diets compatible with one's blood type
- Regular sleep cycles
- Music and art utilization
- Play therapy
- Hot baths and long showers
- Prayer and meditation
- Violence prevention programs
- Tai Chi for veterans in combat zones who experience PTSD

- Y Kids Healthy Day Program
- Trauma amelioration program e.g., United Black Funds "I Love Life Campaign" which helps youth overcome trauma arising from community and family problems
- New paradigms for treatment e.g., FDA agreement for new trials for ecstasy to sooth PTSD
- Community members participation in ending gun violence (e.g., a trauma patient who pushed for gun violence studies relative to guns and neighborhoods beset by competitive street gangs)
- Community programs that end gun violence
- Family, mental health fairs and expos
- Call to Healthy Summits (Baltimore Mental Health Association)
- Walter Reed's program to help PTSD and traumatic brain injury (TBI) by encouraging patients to paint their emotions on masks (reference to art and music activities)
- Use of relevant films (e.g., "Unnatural Cause: When the Bough Breaks")
- Emotional Emancipation Circles – self-help support groups for black people to heal from race-based trauma (originated by Community Healing Network, Inc.)
- Use of light and imaging to treat Posttraumatic Stress Disorders (University of Texas at Arlington)
- Psychotherapy for traumatic stress after hurricanes (American Psychological Association)
- Research and develop prescribed medication for PTSD and other trauma
- Upgrade trauma care units at hospitals and clinics
- A program called "In the Mountains" (a week-long

retreat or respite for war veterans)
- Respite centers for traumatized youth
- Refuse to let past childhood sexual abuse trauma poison the future
- Manage traumatic stress after hurricanes or natural disasters
- Avoid dwelling on past stressful events
- Use art, journaling and videos for managing intrusive traumatic material and dissociations
- Manage safety struggles, and work through attachment difficulties
- Parents need to notice PTSD in their children and also recognize their own need for support
- Review Stanford University's School of Medicine's study of trauma and its impact on the brains of adolescent boys and girls
- Use of dogs and other pets for therapy
- Confront traumatic memory either as self-help or in group and community therapy
- Research, review and attend relevant workshops (e.g., "Trauma, Affect, Dysregulation and Shame: Treating the Seeds of Self- Destructive Behavior")

II. Violence

VIOLENCE is any type of behavior involving physical force intended to hurt, damage or kill someone or something. Types of violence include: criminal violence, domestic violence, gang and police as well as severe abuses. Examples:

Criminal Violence – Burglary, robbery, rape, and homicide

Domestic Violence – Physical abuse, mental and emotional abuse, sexual abuse stalking or cyberstalking

Gang Violence – Criminal and non-criminal political acts of violence committed by a group of people who regularly engage in criminal activity against innocent people; physical, hostile interaction between two or more people organized to achieve a common objective (e.g., oppression, suppression and vilification), and who share a common identity

Police Violence (also known as police brutality) – The use of unnecessary, excessive force beyond what is needed to handle a situation. Forms of police violence include physical abuse (e.g., beating), nerve gas, pepper spray and shooting to hurt civilians. Police brutality also consists of false arrest, sexual abuse, unlawful stop, search and seizure, racial profiling, and police corruption (re: Baltimore and Chicago reports from the office of the former Attorney General Loretta Lynch).

Media Violence – Visual portrayals of acts of physical aggression by one human or human-like character against another. (Example: Bandura Study on media violence, the Bobo Dolls and "The Godfather" movie series).

Idiopathic Violence – Externalizing disorders, conduct and anti-social behavior disorder. Examples: anger, i.e., going from grumpiness to rage which relates to intensity and purpose, emotions and behaviors (*New York Times* article by Barrett, November 12, 2016: "The Varieties of Anger").

School Violence – It includes violence between school students as well as physical attacks by students on school staff and vice versa.

Cyber Bullying – Bullying that takes place using electronic technology. Electronic technology includes devices and equipment such as cell phones, computers, and tablets as well as communication tools including social media sites, text messages, chat, and websites.

Recommendations:

Criminal Violence

- Incarceration
- Education
- Employment opportunities
- Gun laws rather than same stereotype from public (e.g., fear and endless discussion about how we can keep it from re-occurring)
- Stop the revolving door for violent offenders
- Data driven policies
- Ban all combat-type weapons from our communities

Domestic Violence

- Call the police when you hear evidence of domestic violence
- Refer people to a domestic violence outreach program
- Educate others on domestic violence (civic organizations, religious or faith-based organizations, workplace and school)
- Model respect and healthy relationships for children and others
- Encourage and develop neighborhood watch and block associations
- Seek legal aid and advice from family law attorneys
- Regulate mandatory reporters: doctors, dentists, clergy and school officials
- Provide restraining orders: emergency protection, temporary restraining orders and domestic violence restraining orders
- Obtain domestic violence information for your state:
  - National Domestic Violence Hotline
  - Domestic Violence Organizations
  - Domestic Violence Resources
- World Health Organization and Center for Disease Control (CDC) team up to end violence against children
- Deal with spiritual component of violence
- Work with domestic violence activists to create safe havens and bring social services into troubled homes and relationships
- Provide services to ex-offenders to help them become productive citizens in order to prevent recurring violence

- Use media, (e.g., the film "The Burning Bed") for educational purposes

Gang Violence

- Youth development programs with emphases on employability skills development, economic empowerment and positive self-esteem
- Recreational activities
- Counseling and psychotherapy
- Mentoring programs
- Sport camps and retreats
- Tutorial programs
- Working with juvenile centers
- Crisis intervention services
- Police, court, and social services advocacy initiatives
- Community-based direct services and outreach programs
- Support groups for victims of hate crimes, violence and abuse
- Gang violence prevention curricula
- Conflict management and resolution
- Develop comprehensive training and education programs for community members, police, courts, school, rape crisis centers and domestic violence organizations to work as collaborative and cooperative partners
- National Gang Intelligence Center (NGIC)
- Gang Resistance Education and Training (GREAT) Program

- U.S. Department of Juvenile Justice and Delinquency Prevention (OJJDP) programs and resources

Police Violence (Example: a police sergeant shot a mentally ill woman because he did not follow his training)

- Prioritize community policing
- Limit police intervention
- Improve community interactions
- Advocate for changes in existing policies and procedures
- Ensure accountability
- Require police officers to undergo training including:
    - Racial bias and diversity
    - Crisis intervention
    - Mediation
    - Conflict resolution
    - Modern training relating to "here and now" situations and circumstances
- Teach children to respect police officers and how to communicate with them
- Build partnerships to develop and implement visible engagement programs:
    - Neighborhood police academy for youth and adults
    - Sport teams
    - Police-led community events
    - Kids ride-along with police

Media Violence

- Reduce the over exposure to violence on TV and in movies
- Replicate United Black Fund programs to get rid of weapons of mass destruction and push for a culture of non-violence
- Develop a national anti-violence program for children and adolescents modeled after "Sesame Street"
- Create anti-exposure preventive measures to keep children from being exposed to or have access to violence programs
- Support federal and local governments, communities and family plans; promote and implement programs and projects to regulate media violence
- Cooperate with major organizations (e.g., churches, businesses, civic and social) to sponsor anti-violence programs and projects

Idiopathic Violence

- Research for a brain-based understanding of difficult and aggressive behaviors
- Develop brain imaging for a deeper understanding of violence, to reduce stigma, increase compliances and improve outcomes
- Promote laissez-faire approaches and exhaustion techniques for children who are having fiery

temper tantrums
- Find the root cause of violence in a child, let the child get the feelings out in a safe way; keep all in the home safe and be a steady parent as the child struggles
- Teach the child ways to handle emotions
- Help children avoid displaced hatred in order to prevent self-injury or worse

School Violence

- Raise healthy kids, start with compassion, we need them to love and be kind to themselves and others for who they are
- Research to get a brain-based understanding of difficult and aggressive behavior
- Advocate for children to wear the same uniforms with no to minor exceptions
- Promote community control of schools (e.g., school authorities are those who have been members of the community where they are working)
- Hire teachers and school personnel from the local or compatible community

III. Substance Abuse

ALCOHOL misuse and abuse cause distress or harm. It ultimately leads to alcoholism and many related problems.

Recommendations:

- Begin with honesty and truth (e.g., "I, my spouse, relative, child or friend has a drinking problem and it's out of control.")
- Seek help
- Examine and select a treatment option:
    - Alcohol counseling (behavioral treatment) with a health professional. Types include: motivational enhancement therapy, cognitive – behavioral therapy, marital and family counseling as well as other interventions
    - Mutual support groups such as Alcoholics Anonymous with a 12-Steps Program
    - Inpatient rehabilitation (28 days residential)
    - Food and Drug Administration (FDA) approved medication
- Obtain advice from trusted family members and friends
- Be persistent: "if at first you don't succeed, try and try again!"
- Remove all temptations
- Distance yourself from drinking buddies and bad influences
- Attend a detoxification center
- Don't use alcohol to manage stress
- Expand coverage for alcohol treatment
- Utilize the alcoholism programs of the National Association for the Mentally Ill (NAMI)

NARCOTICS unless prescribed by a licensed medical expert are dangerous and deadly. There are four broad categories: (1) opioids and opioid-like agents (codeine, morphine and heroine; (2) cannabinoids (hashish and marijuana); (3) hallucinogens (phencyclidine i.e., PCP or Angel Dust); and (4) stimulants. Some of the top drugs include: cocaine, crack, heroin, LSD, opium, Ritalin and steroids.

Recommendations:

- Drug knowledge, education and intergenerational training (i.e., children, youth, adults and grandparents)
- Train police in their role of responding to the opioid situations and crises
- Provide individual and group counseling and psychotherapy
- Develop comprehensive drug addiction treatment services
  - Mental health
  - Medical
  - Vocational
  - Family
  - Educational
  - Legal
- Utilize recovery support programs (e.g., Narcotics Anonymous)
- Research the effects of medical marijuana and its reduction of opioid prescriptions
- Promote government policies to help stamp out the opioid epidemic
- Establish faith-based organizations to support elimination of the opioid crisis
- Build drug recovery high schools
- Provide continuing care

- Design drug awareness programs
- Develop holistic addiction treatment techniques
- Use social media to educate families and family support groups (e.g., the Narconon Program)
- Follow medical guidelines for treatment of chronic pain with medications
- Keep hope alive with one's life philosophy and spirituality
- Establish Overdose Alert Programs (e.g., Baltimore City)

IV. Suicide

SUICIDE is a desperate attempt to escape suffering that has become unbearable because of such feelings as hopelessness, isolation, depression and self-loathing. They want whatever pain they're in to stop!

Recommendations:

- Be proactive and do not ignore threats or actions
- Get professional help, counseling and psychotherapy
- Talk about problems and concerns with a friend or trusted family member
- Call a crisis line for advice and referrals
- Promote and help the person to develop a positive life style, healthy diet, adequate sleep, exercise and time in the sun or with nature.
- Be alert to triggers that may lead to a suicidal crisis (e.g., death of a loved one, alcohol, stress and broken relationships)

- Parents, teachers and others should be available and listen attentively
- Remove those things that can be used for suicides: knives, razors, firearms and medications that can be used to overdose.
- Encourage friendships and recreation
- Seek spiritual advice and guidance
- Wikipedia recommends the following:[97]
    - Developing groups led by professionally trained individuals for broad-based support for suicide prevention
    - Promoting community-based suicide prevention programs
    - Screening and reducing at-risk behavior through psychological resilience programs that promote optimism and connectedness
    - Education about suicide, including risk factors, warning signs, stigma related issues and the availability of help through social campaigns
    - Increasing the proficiency of health and welfare services responding to people in need. e.g., sponsored training for helping professionals, increased access to community linkages and employing crisis counseling organizations
    - Reducing domestic violence and substance abuse through legal and empowerment means as long-term strategies
    - Reducing access to convenient means of suicide and

---

[97] For additional insight, read *Black Suicide* by Herbert Hendin who used psychoanalytic interviewing techniques to study and report twenty-five black patients who made suicide attempts and share the general pressures, conflicts, frustrations and anger of their life in the black ghetto.

methods of self-harm (e.g., toxic substances, poisons and handguns)

- Reducing the quantity of dosages supplied in packages of non-prescription medicines (e.g., aspirin)
- School-based competency promoting programs
- Interventions and usage of ethical surveillance systems targeted at high-risk groups
- Improving reporting and portrayals of negative behavior, suicidal behavior, mental illness and substance abuse in the entertainment and news media (e.g., Netflix's series: "13 Reasons Why")
- Research on protective factors and development of effective clinical and professional practices
- Prioritize suicide prevention at Veterans Administration
- Develop suicide prevention strategies for working with lesbians, gay, bisexual, transgender (LGBT) youth

Miseducation Concerns and Recommendations

1. Understanding African American Heritage and the African American Spirit

We have a rich heritage and unconquerable spirit. It has not been comprehensively understood, documented, or taught in our schools and colleges the way American history has, and nor has it been a priority. During the 1950s, understanding African American heritage became a priority because nothing and no one could keep us down after Brown vs. The Board of Education. We need to let the world know, and teach our families and children, how we survived, how we thrive and how we can still rise -- against all odds.

Recommendations:

- Provide adequate financial resources to teach African American history and culture
- Teach African American history: Do not water it down
- Read books about African American history. Learn the history
- Celebrate African American history daily by referencing examples of pioneers, their works and contributions Learn them, quote them and apply their teachings
- Visit museums (e.g., The new African American Museum in Washington, DC)
- Anti-Defamation League[98] recommends:
    - Read and discuss black literature
    - Identify and investigate important periods in black history
    - Explore black art
    - Learn about important people in black history
    - Watch and discuss films about the black experience
    - Listen to black music
    - Learn about black migration and immigration

---

[98] Anti-Defamation League (ADL). (2013). 10 Ideas for Teaching Black History Month. Retrieved from ADL: http://www.adl.org/assets/pdf/education-outreach/10-ideas-for-teaching-black-history-month.pdf

- Classify and take action on the civil rights issues of our times
- Talk about racism and discrimination
- Research the origins of black history month

- Make some readings required for all students. Examples:
  - *The Miseducation of the Negro* – Carter G. Woodson
  - *Before the Mayflower* – Lerone Bennett, Jr.
  - *The Destruction of Black Civilization* – Chancellor Williams
  - *Afrocentricity* – Dr. Molefi Kete Asante
  - *Black Rage* – W. H. Grier and P. M. Cobbs
  - *The Isis Papers* – Dr. Francis Welsing
  - *Even the Rats Were White* – Robert Guthrie

2. Poor Schools

Schools serving poor and minority students do not have the variety or resources that they need to educate the disadvantage students they serve. High-poverty schools need more than financial resources to improve student learning.

Recommendations:

- Encourage community control of schools
- Provide early childhood education services or programs beginning at age three
- Make "No Child Left Behind" a reality
- Provide adequate financial resources
- Hire teachers skilled in working with diverse and at-risk student populations

- Involve parents in all aspects of their child's education
- Encourage schools to provide healthy snack options
- Enhance, empower and expand Parent Teacher Association (PTA)
- Hire clinical psychologists to work with urban schools
- Provide school-based mental health centers with highly qualified staff
- Form partnerships with major community-based organizations, law enforcement, youth detention centers, hospitals and faith-based organizations
- Provide after school tutorial and counseling programs
- Provide cultural enrichment activities and programs
- Use community leaders as role models and guest speakers
- Use local college professors to visit and lecture in various classes
- Provide writing centers at all high schools
- Develop a "buddy system" between high school students and college students for academic support

- Develop opportunities for students after high school— especially those who are not going to college
- Help schools improve the quality of their standard operating practices
- Increase the instructional capacity of staff in schools through professional development or more selective hiring
- Enhance incentives and provide local actors more flexibility through policies such as school choice or accountability
- Develop a cooperative partnership between principals, teachers, parents, coaches and mentors
- Develop school-wide support classroom

programs with a student achievement focus
- Encourage community organizations to work together to benefit the schools
- Provide computer-assisted instruction and tutoring tools for students and parents

3. Lack of Opportunities After High School

Research studies have found that many students do not have plans beyond high school, particularly those who are not going to college for whatever reason. Some reasons for their indecision include not having resources needed for a post-secondary education or training and limited options for employment and simply not knowing what to do.

Recommendations:

- Encourage local businesses to develop programs and jobs for high school students who are not going to college
- Increase vocational training opportunities
- Design internship programs that can lead to employment or transition to college
- Promote entrepreneurship and small business development
- Explore and consider military opportunities
- Volunteer to serve community and faith-based organizations
- Attend technical or trade school
- Develop marketable skills for use in the world of work
- Learn about blue collar job opportunities
- Seek internships

- Consider viable on-the-job training
- Utilize mentoring for job opportunities
- Receive coaching while on the job
- Seek livable wages and opportunities for career advancement
- Explore the job market and career opportunities

Poverty Concerns and Recommendations

1. Impoverished Families

Impoverished families live below the federal poverty threshold (a measurement that has been shown to underestimate the needs of families), earn low wages, and some have unstable employment which leave their families struggling to make ends meet. Poverty can impede their children's ability to learn, and it contributes to social, emotional, and behavioral problems as well as poor health and mental health.

Recommendations:

- Review and expand The Working Poor Families Project (WPFP), a national initiative focused on state workforce development policies involving: 1) education and skills training for adults; 2) economic development; and 3) income and work supports. The WPFP supports state nonprofit groups to engage in a two-part, phased process that begins with an in-depth assessment of the economic conditions and state policies affecting working families, and it is followed by actions to strengthen those

184

conditions and policies

- Explore federal assistance programs to lift people, including children, out of poverty and provide access to affordable health care
- Encourage the use of programs like Supplemental Nutrition Assistance Program (SNAP -- food stamps), the Earned Income Tax Credit (EITC), Cost to Company (CTC), and Medicaid support
- Seek low-income housing
- Explore and obtain job training
- Seek educational assistance
- Obtain financial aid for the disabled
- Expand food banks
- Encourage people to double their savings for retirement
- Develop public housing policies that encourage and support home ownership
- Allow more people with disabilities to live in community environments rather than institutional settings
- Provide shelters for homeless populations
- Eliminate the rent burdens of the urban poor
- Increase home loans to African Americans who are seeking home ownership
- Provide long-term subsidies for the homeless until they are able to fend for themselves
- Create adequate day care for those who are in school
- Provide a strong safety net for the poor
- Create family emergency funds for unexpected events (e.g., death of head of household, unemployment, health problems)

- Promote policy on the rising sea levels and emissions that increase risks to residents of our cities
- Provide financial resources for grandparents who are caring for their children's children who need adequate support
- Rent public housing to those with absolute needs
- Establish general support for ex-inmates
- Make cities viable for ex-inmates
- Provide food subsidies and programs for needy families and their children
- Eliminate discrimination in housing
- Encourage landlords to accept applicants with a criminal past
- Advocate that libraries make provisions for helping the poor (e.g., digital access)
- Encourage local government to provide housing for the homeless, minimizing placement in hotels
- Establish gender parity through jobs
- Maintain consumer protection agency boards
- Provide adequate employment opportunities to reduce moonlighting
- Establish policies to keep the gentrification of cities from having continued negative impacts on the poor
- Coordinate affordable housing and transit systems
- Compensate workers with time and one-half for all overtime work performed
- Implement programs to take care of the poor (e.g., food banks, civic and faith-based initiatives)
- Reduce and eliminate teen birth rates
- Eliminate public housing

- Allow schools to control their own feeding programs subject to their community-school control boards
- Mandate universal health care
- Encourage all able-bodied adults to gain full employment and or a viable activity
- Implement rent controls for low-income tenants
- Adjust housing cost to lead to healthy population flows
- Remove structural barriers that have kept African Americans from accumulating wealth
- Educate and train Blacks to take leadership in all anti-poverty initiatives
- Utilize a "whole-child" approach to education that will help to break the cycle of poverty
- Invest in health and wellness programs and projects
- Develop social and emotional skills
- Encourage employers to share profits with their workers
- Obtain career or technical skills and certifications
- Increase community-agency dialogues
- Develop a unified approach to holistic education
- Expand the middle class again by income equality (e.g., "share the wealth")
- Eliminate the wage gap between black and white educated workers
- Plant community gardens to help poor kids eat garden crops with a variety of choices
- Recognize and prepare for the impact that disasters (e.g., tornadoes, hurricanes and floods) have on the poor
- Adjust the rent for large families (six or more individuals in household)
- Reduce welfare rolls by helping people gain viable

employment in non-welfare status

- Provide jobs and humane punishment to deter crime
- Provide resources for childcare workers who are in poverty as they care for other poor children
- Balance the ability of poor people to live throughout their ecosystem
- Institute government programs to end poverty
- Pay attention to the poverty in small town America and integrate it into overall planning and programming
- Develop programs for the aging populations
- Focus on housing as a central means of helping to end poverty
- Establish a minimum wage that will support a family of four
- End hunger in America for all groups and provide proper nutrition for everyone
- Keep local communities strong to help end poverty
- Provide paid family leave as a rule throughout the nation
- Use the internet to help poor and working-class families (e.g., Craig's List)
- Develop programs for at-risk young people
- Remove child care barriers for parents seeking employment
- Utilize indices that adjusts for the cost of raising a child (e.g., the cost of raising a child increased 3% in 2015)
- Require black unemployment to match that of whites (e.g., the job data as of 2016 indicated that white unemployment was 4.3%, Black 7.8% and Hispanic 5.9%)

2. Lack of Jobs for Ex-Felons

Ex-felons can often have a hard time finding employment after incarceration. The "system" traditionally has not considered them to be viable candidates for employment. To add to that, many felons become discouraged because of their perceptions of how society views them, coupled with their lack of knowledge and understanding, as well as skills to obtain and maintain a job. Nevertheless, there are some options available.

Recommendations:

- Encourage local organizations to partner with businesses to create programs and services (e.g., counseling, employability skills and transition to the world of work programs) for felons
- Research the opportunities that government programs and privately run charities provide to assist felons
- Seek and join local support groups to get useful advice on finding and tracking jobs
- Find reentry programs and reentry websites that are good places to check when looking for a job
- Contact faith-based organizations and their services and programs for ex-offenders
- Explore construction companies that offer jobs and skills training for felons: tile, carpentry, electrical, plumbing, welding, pipe fitting, carpet, HVAC and roofing
- Choose landscaping as a career
- Hire felons as truck drivers if allowed by law

- Contact fast food restaurants that are felon-friendly: McDonalds, Burger King, Subway, Taco Bell, Hardees, Red Robin, Dairy Queen and Baskin Robins
- Seek help for felony expungement
- Join ex-felon self-help groups
- Ensure that government policies promote communal reentry for ex-felons (e.g., full voting rights and other rights restored)
- Provide social support for ex-felons (e.g., psychological coaching, mentoring, and illumination psychotherapy)
- Utilize government, small businesses and successful entrepreneurships to provide support to help ex-felons establish and develop small businesses

3. Dearth of Small Business

As big businesses and conglomerates grow, small black businesses continue to decline. In urban communities, many of these small businesses have gone or are going out of business. Therefore, there is a need for small black businesses to reinvent themselves and provide new goods and services to their communities.

Recommendations:

- Make small business development a high priority
- Provide entrepreneurship courses in public schools
- Utilize the resources of the Small Business Administration (SBA)

- Gain a fair share of federal and local government contracts
- Encourage people to shop at small black businesses in their communities
- Support small businesses in the community: restaurants, hair salons, nail salons, barbershops, laundromats, etc.
- Purchase from specialty stores catering to specific ethnicities or nationalities
- Find a mentor who is knowledgeable and skilled in establishing black businesses
- Learn as much as you can about the business that you want to develop
- Find successful models of various businesses of interest to you or that will benefit your community
- Explore financing and where the money is coming from
- Hold on to your dreams!

4. Poor Access to Transportation

Transportation is needed for inner-city residents to go where they need to in order to receive services and have quality lives. It's hard for those living in poverty to access jobs, resources and good schools. Transportation is more than just moving people from point A to point B. It is also a system that can either limit or expand the opportunities available to people based on where they live. Therefore, many inner-city residents are compromised when it means acquiring employment, accessing medical care, obtaining groceries and engaging in recreational activities.

Recommendations:

- Provide transportation for all segments of the community
- Meet travel demands
- Provide timely schedules
- Operate transportation services at critical periods
- Hire people from the local community to operate the transportation system at all levels
- Make sure that the fares for transportation are affordable for all users
- Provide excellent customer service to all

5. Poor Nutrition

Nutrition is vital to healthy and wholesome living. Good nutrition is one of the keys to good health. Unfortunately, good nutrition is seldom taught and practiced in the homes of the urban poor. The most systematic and efficient means for improving the health and life styles of families and communities is to teach nutrition, healthy dietary habits and physical activity. Moreover, teaching nutrition education may be a major factor in preventing childhood obesity. Research reports that poor nutrition plagues as many as one in three children in America. Many of these children will suffer from a plethora of potential health complications and issues, as well as several social and emotional complications, such as low self-esteem, behavioral and learning problems and depression.

Recommendations:

- Establish a nutrition education program for all schools
- Integrate nutrition information across the school's curricula
- Review and utilize Michelle Obama's programs and activities relating to obesity and replicate some of them (e.g., youth gardens at school)
- Hold seminars and workshops for parents in schools and in community-based and faith-based organizations
- Peruse the brief history of USDA Food Guidelines (www.choosemyplate.gov)
- Learn the importance of using certain spices which can be a school or community project. Some common spices include:

  - **Cinnamon**: Can lower blood sugar, triglycerides, LDL, and total cholesterol in people with type 2 diabetes.
  - **Turmeric**: Contains curcumin, which can inhibit the growth of cancer cells
  - **Rosemary**: Stops gene mutations that could lead to cancer and may help prevent damage to the blood vessels that raise heart attack risk
  - **Garlic**: Destroys cancer cells and may disrupt the metabolism of tumor cells
  - **Paprika**: Contains capsaicin, whose anti-inflammatory and antioxidant effects may lower the risk of cancer (also found in cayenne and red chili peppers)
  - **Ginger**: Can decrease motion sickness and nausea; may also relieve pain and swelling associated with arthritis

- Get involved with the USDA and Food and Nutrition Service (FNS) resources designed to provide tools needed to conduct effective nutrition education:
  - MyPlate (www.choosemyplate.gov) offers tips and resources designed to educate on how incorporating the dietary guidelines into your diet can lead to a healthier you
  - Team Nutrition (www.fns.usda.gov/tn/team-nutrition) provides nutrition education for kids and their caregivers. Inside, you'll find a comprehensive listing of materials designed for food service professionals, educators, parents, and child care providers
  - Supplemental Nutrition Assistance Program (SNAP)-Ed Connection (www.snaped.fns.usda.gov/national-snap-ed) has tools to help people stretch their food dollars. The site includes handouts and curricula. There are also materials for educators
  - The Let's Move! Initiative (letsmove.obamawhitehouse.archives.gov) gives parents and caregivers the educational resources they need to make healthy choices for children
- Teach children and parents how to read food labels in schools and in community based organizations
- Start a healthy cooking club
- Visit local farmers markets or produce stores
- Use blood types to establish nutritional plans

6. Lack of Recreational Facilities

Studies show that African American adolescents are disproportionately overweight or obese, and that these conditions are linked to a lack of physical activity. A number of neighborhood attributes play a role in discouraging people in low-income areas from participating in physical activity. Many low-income communities lack access to parks and recreation areas.

Recommendations:

- Develop partnerships with various local organizations, schools, and businesses to help run or house athletic or exercise programs
- Provide public recreational facilities and programs
- Advocate for federal, state and local governments to develop funding streams and affordable opportunities for recreational facilities and programs in urban communities
- Utilize the available space in local community parks
- Utilize church parking lots for structured and scheduled outdoor recreational activities
- Create community-based recreational programs for teens
- Promote afterschool recreational activities (e.g., sports, board games and clubs)
- Obtain community control of recreational organizations and programs
- Select leaders who develop recreational activities that promote the black experience and achievement
- Make sure that recreational experience is holistic as it

relates to personal growth and development
- Provide recognition and awards for achievements
- Engage the entire community in programming processes

After the recommendations and solutions were presented, followed by a question and answer period, the session ended. The audience's engagement with the panelists, suggestions and recommendations made throughout the afternoon, and the entire Summit were excellent.

Unfortunately, Professor Johnson had to end the session while the audience was in high gear and wanted more. However, time was up. So, he explained the agenda for the next day.

First, he said, "Spirituality is our last topic and it is befitting for us to discuss it tomorrow at our closing session. It will be a breakfast with guest speaker, Rev. Dr. Thurman Smith, author of the best seller, *Understanding Spirituality*. I am sure you will be enlightened and uplifted."

Second, he asked all of the participants to meet, brainstorm and summarize the Summit, and to be prepared to report back to the entire audience. He directed community participants to Conference Room A; the students to Conference Room B; and Grandma Johnson and her children to Conference Room C.

Third, he told the audience that the mayor and he would give their final remarks at the Summit finale.

"Thank you for being a wonderful audience. Enjoy your

evening and continue to be blessed."

SUNDAY MORNING: Spirituality and the Summit Finale

An impressive buffet breakfast was prepared by The Best is Yet to Come Caterers, a local faith-based inner city company that specializes in weddings, conferences and other civic-social functions. The menu consisted of: pancakes, waffles, a French toast casserole, oatmeal, grits, a variety of eggs, turkey bacon and sausage, ham, spinach quiche, pastries and their signature dish, "Shakshuka" (North African eggs in spicy tomato sauce). The buffet also had a juice bar.

The mistress of ceremony for breakfast was Judy Thompson, one of Professor Johnson's students and president of the university's Student Government Association. She started by greeting the audience, and then she asked the blessing. Everyone selected their food, beverages, and their seats and began to eat.

Judy then introduced Rev. Dr. Thurman Smith. She said, "We are fortunate, no blessed, to have a great speaker this morning, Rev. Dr. Thurman Smith. Dr. Smith is a graduate of Morehouse College where he received his B.A. in Political Science; he received a Master's in Public Administration from Emory University and a Doctorate in Ministry from Boston University. He is a retired military chaplain with more than 25 years of experience in religious services and counseling in hospitals, prisons, police stations and universities. He has travelled all over the world, currently serves on several boards of directors, writes best-selling books, and his articles appear in refereed journals and popular magazines. He also volunteers at faith-based and community organizations and does much more.

Ladies and gentlemen put your forks or spoons down, or your coffee or tea and let's give a warm welcome to Rev. Dr. Thurman Smith—show him some love!"

Dr. Smith greeted the audience with a big, infectious grin. "Thank you for the love" he said. "I greet you with the love of the Lord and first give Him honor. I thank my dear friend, Professor Johnson, for inviting me to participate in this outstanding Family and Community Empowerment Summit, and I thank each of you who thought it not robbery to invest your time, share with each other and learn from all of the experts here—to God be the glory!

"I will not stand before you very long because I like to KISS (Keep It Short and Sweet) and BS (Be Seated), he chuckled. "Professor Johnson asked me to share some thoughts on spirituality. He also gave me a 'carte blanche' which I will graciously use and talk about three things: (1) definitions of spirituality; (2) biblical perspectives of spirituality; and (3) the importance of spirituality and spiritual growth to health.

"First of all, I want you to think about the word spirituality for a few minutes, Dr. Smith said. What is spirituality? What are some prevalent conceptualizations?, he asked. These are not rhetorical questions; however, let me tell you some of the things that I did when I was researching and writing my latest book, *Understanding Spirituality*. I started with my usual approach to any subject, i.e., to define it first. I looked for what the bible says about spirituality, and a quick search gave me thirty verses about spirituality in general, but not a definition. So, I continued my search. Meanwhile, my pastor-friend, Rev. Joshua Tate called. I told him what I was doing and decided to arbitrarily ask him his definition of spirituality. Joshua seized the opportunity to, so-called 'wax eloquently.'

"He said, 'Spirituality is especially broad and not easy to define because it is multi-dimensional as well as ubiquitous. Everybody can chime in as to what is defined as spirituality. It can be defined by the deeply religious as a being or force that is transcendent or omnipresent. It can be defined by the less religious as something that assigns kinship with all nature—animals, babies, plants, etc. Who's to decide? How can we agree on something that affords each of us the inclination to say what is spirituality verses what is not spirituality? As a professing Christian and passionate admirer of a lot of things academic, I like the National Center for Cultural Competence's definition of spirituality.'

He said:

> Spirituality refers to a broad set of principles and beliefs that transcend all religions. Spirituality is about the relationship between ourselves and something larger. That something can be the good of the community or the people who are served by your agency or school or with energies greater than ourselves. Spiritualty means being in the right relationship with all that is. It is a stance of harmless toward all living beings and an understanding of

their mutual interdependence.[99]

"As an African-American Baptist pastor, preacher and community organizer, I can describe spirituality in terms of how our folks got over and brothers and sisters of faith and well-meaning persons of every description raise up standards for justice, peace, and fairness in the land. I am reminded of a definition of spirituality by Rev. Dr. Freddie Barnes: "Spirituality is deeply personal—both in philosophical concepts as well as a praxis that directs and informs all I espouse and try to be about.[100]

"Then, my wife interrupted and told me that lunch was ready, and I had to get off the phone with Joshua. I thanked him for his insight, and told him that 'Wifey' was calling me to lunch, and I had to run.

"Can I quote you in my book?" I asked.

He said, "Sure can. Don't forget to send me a copy. Blessings to you and the first lady."

"Back at cha, Bro, later, I said to him and ended the call.

"I shared this with you because Joshua was a big inspiration to me and actually helped me to simplify the conceptual framework for my book and hence what I want to share with you. As promised, I am going to KISS (Keep It Short and Sweet) and BS (Be Seated)

---

[99] Kaiser, L. (2000) "Spirituality and the Physician Executive: Reconciling the Inner Self and the Business of Health Care" The Physician Executive. 26(2) March/April
[100] Rev. Dr. Freddie Barnes (Goldsboro, N.C.)

starting with simple definitions of spirituality.

"According to Mario Beauregard and Denyse O'Leary, researchers and authors of *The Spiritual Brain*, 'spirituality means any experience that is thought to bring the experiencer into contact with the divine (in other words, not just any experience that feels meaningful).' Christina Puchalski, MD, Director of the George Washington Institute for Spirituality and Health, contends that 'spirituality is the aspect of humanity that refers to the way individuals seek and express meaning and purpose and the way they experience their connectedness to the moment, to self, to others, to nature and to the significant or sacred.'[101]

"Researchers theorize that there are four components of spirituality: belief, practice, awareness and experience. Let me briefly explain each component.

1. Belief- An assent to or conviction about a domain or existence that goes beyond the material world. This includes all manner of religious or other beliefs that are not based on materialism.

2. Practice- Spiritual or religious practice at this level occurs without conscious awareness of, or relationship to, the spiritual realm addressed. Although it involves exercises of imagination and desire such as contemplation, prayer, reading or reflection, the self is not moved by any direct experience of relationship

---

[101] University of Minnesota. (n.d.). What is Spirituality? Retrieved from Taking Charge of Your Health and Well-Being: https://www.takingcharge.csh.umn.edu/what-spirituality

with or connection to the other.

3. Awareness- There is an awareness of being moved intellectually and/or emotionally. It includes contemplation, prayer, meditation or reflection when there is conscious awareness of, or response to, this dimension.

4. Experience- A discrete experience which may include diffusion of the mind, loss of ego boundaries and a change in orientation from self towards or beyond the material world. The experience usually comes unbidden but may follow a period of reflection, meditation, stress or isolation. Ecstatic experiences are of this type, but experience may be much less intense and more prolonged.[102]

"I want to also point out seven spiritual needs or spiritual hungers which I have adapted from research by Howard Clinebell:

1. People need to experience healing and empowerment of love from a variety of sources including the Creator
2. People need time for transcendent renewal
3. People need beliefs that provide hope in the midst of tragedies, losses and failures
4. People need values, priorities and commitments based on integrity and love in order to have a wholesome living lifestyle
5. People need to develop wisdom and self-love

---

[102] http://www.biomedcental.com/1472-6963/9/116

202

6. People need to connect with other people and all living things
7. People need spiritual resources for healing and to help eliminate negativisms, and they need to practice living the fruit of the spirit: love, joy, peace, forbearance (patience), kindness, goodness, faithfulness, gentleness and self-control.[103]

Dr. Smith said, "It is imperative that I emphasize the role of the church. Since the times of slave masters dropping bibles down to shackled Africans who couldn't read or speak the English language—black people have always developed a deeply personal definition of God and their spiritual identity. Enduring extreme persecution and exploitation, black people took a template of Christianity and customized it to reflect their own interpretation of its teachings. As a result, spirituality became the soul of our artistry, the language of our existence, and the back bone of our communities. It instilled a sense of power and purpose within a race of people who were deemed powerless.[104]

"Spirituality is our belief and connection to something bigger than ourselves. That something is God. God is the source of our strength and our deliverer. Lamentations 2:22-24 tells us, 'It is of the Lord's mercies that we are not consumed because His compassions fail not; they are new every morning: great is thy faithfulness. The Lord is my portion saith my soul; therefore will I

[103] University of Minnesota. (n.d.). Seven Spiritual Needs. Retrieved from Taking Charge of Your Health & Well-Being: https://www.takingcharge.csh.umn.edu/enhance-your-wellbeing/purpose/spirituality/seven-spiritual-needs
[104] Mitchell, J. (2015, October 23). God Over Everything: Black Spirituality and the Paradox of Religion. Retrieved from Huffington Post: http://www.huffingtonpost.com/Julian-mitchell/god-over-everything-

hope in Him.' The songwriter, Thomas Chilsom, pinned the song, 'Great is Thy Faithfulness' which can be considered a testament to spirituality."

Great is Thy Faithfulness[105]

Great is Thy faithfulness, O God my Father;
There is no shadow of turning with Thee,
Thou changest not, Thy compassions they fail not, As
Thou hast been, Thou forever wilt be.

Great is Thy faithfulness! Great is Thy faithfulness!
Morning by morning new mercies I see
All I have needed Thy hand hath provided
Great is Thy faithfulness, Lord unto me!

Summer and winter and springtime and harvest, Sun,
moon, and stars in their courses above;
Join with all nature in manifold witness,
To Thy great faithfulness, mercy, and love.

Pardon for sin and a peace that endureth,
Thine own dear presence to cheer and to guide;
Strength for today, and bright hope for tomorrow Blessings all
mine, with ten thousand beside.

Great is Thy faithfulness! Great is Thy faithfulness!
Morning by morning new mercies I see;
All I have needed Thy hand hath provided—
Great is Thy faithfulness, Lord, unto me!

---

[105] Wyse, E. (n.d.). The History of "Great is Thy Faithfulness". Retrieved from LifeWay: http://m.lifeway.com/Article/the-history-of-Great-Is-Thy-Faithfulness

"Spirituality has kept us together and will take us out of where we are -- mentally and otherwise." Dr. Smith said, "Spiritualty is now an essential element in healthcare, as Plato noted: 'The cure of the part should not be attempted without the cure of the whole. No attempt should be made to cure the body without the soul and if the head and body are not healthy, you must begin by curing the mind.'[106]

"In closing, I encourage all of you to do some critical thinking about spirituality because spiritual practices are associated with better health and well-being. The medical community strongly advocates medication, coupled with faith in a higher power, to help reduce sensitivity to pain, help regulate emotions, relieve stress, anxiety and depression. Spiritual practices also help people with cancer, fibromyalgia, rheumatoid arthritis, type 2 diabetes, chronic fatigue syndrome, and cardio-vascular disease.[107] Therefore, I leave you with four important takeaways:

1.   Spirituality can give you resilience and strength to overcome life's difficulties and circumstances

2.   Spiritual traditions and a spiritual community of fellowship are support systems which help to provide a sense of belonging and security

3.   Spirituality can help you develop healthy choices (e.g., exercise, not drinking or smoking) and preventive habits

---

[106] Spirituality in Healthcare, (Oxford University Press, 2012)
[107] University of Minnesota. (n.d.). What is Spirituality? Retrieved from Taking Charge of Your Health and Well-Being: https://www.takingcharge.csh.umn.edu/what-spirituality

4. Spirituality is essential to the mission of the Association of Black Psychology

"Finally, my brothers and sisters, always Pray Until Something Happens (PUSH)! Thank you. May God bless and keep you."

The audience gave a resounding applause and a standing ovation as Dr. Smith left the podium, and the loud speaker played BeBe Winan's song, "Let the Church Say Amen." Thereafter, the Family Empowerment Summit groups adjourned to work on their summaries.

GROUP SUMMARIES OF THE SUMMIT

Dr. Johnson reconvened the Summit and asked the groups to make their presentations, which they did.

COMMUNITY PARTICIPANTS gave the Summit tremendous accolades because it gave them a wealth of knowledge about the research findings, existing programs and services, and the unmet needs relating to mental illness, miseducation and poverty. They said the subject matter experts who spoke summarized research and best practices in their field in a manner that was clear, concise and useful. The participants were from every strata of the community and had first-hand knowledge and experience with the negative, impacting forces of the "Three Blind Mice."

They left the conference recognizing the tremendous challenges of the destructive forces prevalent in their communities. The information that they received gave them a head start for planning, programming and evaluating policies for countering mental illness, miseducation and poverty. Each participant pledged to give more time and energy to help establish leadership and memberships in their community groups, to fight for a healthy ecosystem that provides each and every community resident with a feeling of empowerment, trust and control. All groups made commitments to work together, exchange information to keep their communities viable, progressive and illuminated.

PROFESSOR JOHNSON'S STUDENTS were impressed with the information that was presented in a manner that allowed them to process it and digest it for application. They were grateful that they had the opportunity to participate in a challenging forum that tested their ability to formulate solutions to the problems and escalating negative impacts of the "Three Blind Mice". They saw generalizable benefits of the information that they learned: personal growth and development, enhanced personal knowledge, and information that can be useful in various classes, and for their community projects.

The students appreciated the opportunities they had to network with each other and the invited guests. They exchanged ideas and discussed how their education can be used to meet the challenges resulting from the ravages of mental illness, miseducation and poverty. Their desire and commitment are for their education to not be an abstraction but one of unity and positive change. Therefore, the Summit had an illuminated impact on the students and will help to change them from being passive learners to action-oriented ones—ready to do more and give more.

GRANDMA JOHNSON AND HER GRANDCHILDREN were deeply enthralled by the Summit. They all felt very happy to be invited and for the opportunity to attend and learn about the systemic forces of mental illness, miseducation and poverty. They recognized that these forces were operating within their lives and negatively impacting them and their family. Substance abuse and incarceration hit close to home because Grandma Johnson lost her daughter, who is the grandchildren's mother, to alcohol and drugs. The children recognized that they had lost their father to poverty and drug distribution.

The information they gained from the Summit helped to shift their beliefs and increased their knowledge that the black family and black lives matter. The children felt an even closer connection with their grandmother, Aunt Mildred and Uncle John, and a deep sense of rootedness to this primary social group. They expressed determination to reconnect with their mother and father. They also said that they will begin while they are young to help end the scourge of drugs, and help to increase social justice. They will tell their friends all the things they learned.

Grandma Johnson and the children told the audience that their spirituality was heightened with a greater sense of presence of their ancestors. They formed a deeper appreciation of their African heritage. Grandma Johnson also felt more empowered as the matriarch of her family because of the wealth of knowledge she gained from the Summit. She said that she appreciated the fact that she was not alone in raising her grandchildren after raising her child to adulthood. Her love for her brother and sister-in-law deepened their alliance as they helped to raise the children.

Dr. Johnson thanked the groups for their insightful, evaluative and informative summaries. He then invited Mayor Douglas Washington to come forward to give closing remarks and said that he would follow the mayor to close out the Summit.

MAYOR WASHINGTON'S CLOSING REMARKS

"Good afternoon. I want to begin with a big thanks to all of you, for all of the time and energy you invested in masterfully planning and executing this Family and Community Development Empowerment Summit. To all of the politicians, invited guests, educators, authors, speakers and subject matter experts, Dr. Johnson, students and many more that time does not permit me to single out, I again say thank you!

"I would be remiss if I did not take this opportunity to share some insights on how important the scope and content of these sessions have been and how they relate to the gargantuan problems and concerns of cities throughout our nation. For example, the *State of Cities 2016 Report* provides insight into the state of municipal leadership and the issues that matter most to city leaders. The ten top issues are: economic development, public safety, budgets, infrastructure, education, housing, environmental/energy, demographics, data technology and health care.[108]

"The Summit, with your help, has not only provided knowledge and information, it provided solutions and resources. Everything that was said and done is in keeping with the following six trends:

1. Mayors continue to be focused on improving their local economies and encouraging entrepreneurship.
2. Mayors are seeing improved revenue and are being judicious about how to spend it.
3. Mayors are cautiously optimistic about the future and are leading in the development of sustainable communities where people want to live.
4. Mayors are concerned about the uptick in the murder rate even though overall crime rates are historically low.
5. Mayors are concerned about the increasing opioid epidemic.
6. Mayors are helping their cities see the value of using technology and data to drive decisions and make their city governments more efficient and effective.[109]

"I believe we need to utilize a systemic model to construct a city free of the 'Three Blind Mice' and illuminated for all our residents. We need to begin with establishing policies that will mandate the work to be done as well as the processes for sharing responsibilities and receiving necessary feedback. We also need to protect values, interests and the viable programs implemented.

---

[108] National League of Cities. (2016, December 8). State of the Cities 2016. Retrieved from National League of Cities: http://www.nic.org/resource/state-of-the-cities-2016
[109] National League of Cities. (2016, December 8). State of the Cities 2016. Retrieved from National League of Cities: http://www.nic.org/resource/state-of-the-cities-2016

"Policies will direct the city to seek resources state wide, nationally and internationally. They will be necessary to end mental illness, miseducation and poverty (i.e., the 'Three Blind Mice').

"Mental illness must be addressed at the level of the wider society, local community, family and child. Many federal and state agency decisions impact cities, families and children. As mayor, I will see that our community benefits from all resources at the state and federal level. At our level, I will utilize the schools, city agencies and spaces to promote and provide mental health services, recovery and accommodations. Peer-to-peer programs and multi-family programs will take place throughout the city. Various organizations will be invited to participate in collaborative groups to prevent, treat and eliminate mental disorders. Professionals will teach aspects of illumination to psychotherapy associates and educators who can reach a wider audience.

"Emergency services will be fully staffed and ready to address the opioid crisis currently impacting the city. Strong apparatus will be established to rid the city of drugs. Town hall meetings will take place regularly inviting all medical personnel to participate as first responders. All our residents who need treatment will have quality outpatient service to address their needs. With the consultative education programs in all community service agencies and in our schools from Pre-K to grade 12, we envision a parse need for inpatient and partial hospitalization services. All mental health agencies will employ our Community representatives, Administrators, Parents, Teachers and Students (CAPTS) model. Where feasible, families will be given resources to provide high quality care for their members. This entire system of care will be resilient and address the need for diversity.

"Miseducation will be addressed by instituting community control/choice schools that employ indigenous school boards comprised of CAPTS. This composition of the boards will establish transparent mandates and provide resources to address them. We must lobby relevant federal agencies to direct monies (vouchers) for each student enrolled. Resources must be garnered from the state government also. Local funds will be used as well. I will strongly advocate for resources.

"Curricula will promote illumination and lift the blindness of all elements within the constellation of the schools. The schools will be used around the clock to serve the local community, families and children. Each school from Pre-K to grade 12 will have a holistic wellness center to assist with non-academic and academic needs.

"Programs within the wellness center will address all aspects of Maafa enslavement, current issues of physical, mental and spiritual health. Also, it will attend to students and other people affected by violence (e.g., homicide, suicide) and other biopsychosocial problems."

He said, "I recognize this is a bold approach for African Americans trying to thrive in a racist society that once had us in chains on plantations and in other spaces. However, our demand for local control of schools/vouchers will be strong and loud.

"Poverty, DEEP POVERTY, resides in my city and many urban cities at this time. I will bring in my brothers and sisters from the African Diaspora, the federal and state governments to rebuild infrastructures and provide other resources for our city. One of my primary aims will be to have a transportation system that meets the needs of residents for travel demands (e.g., school, work and doctors), and trip-making (e.g., bus, subway and taxis). Travel will be seamless and expeditious.

"I will upgrade our infrastructure to a high quality standard with the use of residents' labor to help with other efforts to meet a zero unemployment goal. As a part of this goal, I will utilize city agencies and programs, licensed neighborhood homes, and family members to provide quality childcare.

"I will strive to make certain that all community systems will work to increase total positive functioning for all residents, for those who need a lot, and for those who need little in services and or care. Public places will be resident friendly and promote relationship building and enhancement. Community gardens, culturally relevant libraries and museums will be part of the new American city.

"I will end my summary by saying the blueprint or plan proffered is to move the city, its families and children from the blindness of mental illness, miseducation and poverty to illumination. Thank you so very much for attending our Summit and may you be blessed as you return and work to illuminate your community. It will take a whole village to keep the light on!"

PROFESSOR JOHNSON

"I want to end our Summit by thanking the Creator of the universe and our source. Like Mayor Washington, I thank all of you. My thanks, our thanks, is extended to so many people who helped to make this Summit a success: we thank the manager and staff of this venue, the hosts and hostesses, caterers, the maintenance team and all of those behind the scene who graciously contributed to this effort. And by the way, didn't my students do an excellent job? Let's all join in and give a big hand clap of thanks and praise.

"I am glad that Mayor Washington gave that brief overview of the *State of Cities Report* which told us what the mayors are trying to do. I, too, want to call your attention to an area that warrants great attention—education.

"Our schools from Pre-K to grade 12 should be the centerpiece of efforts to authentically become illuminated. They should be based on the principles of Kwanzaa and employ the CAPTS model. Foci should be on building resilience, recovering from Posttraumatic Slave Syndrome, developing customs and practices, personal values and quality relationships. There should be emphasis on mindfulness, meditation, exercise, nutrition, empathy and self-compassion. The Summit recommended that an Illumination Psychotherapy Center and Community Empowerment Center be based within the schools. The psycho-emotional task will be balanced with the academic curriculum of Science, Technology, Engineering and Math (STEM) and the humanities. The CAPTS schools will be opened seven days per week and late into the evening to promote reading, special education, community engagement and develop welfare and empowerment.

"We also need the higher education institutions, particularly the historically black colleges and universities (HBCUs) to develop policies, programs and services to meet the needs of our children after they complete their high school education. Traditionally, HBCUs have educated and graduated most students of African descent. There is still an enormous need for their continued standing and viability.

"A recent report, entitled *Top Strategic Issues Facing HBCUs Now and into the Future,* (written by the Association of Governing Boards of Universities and Colleges) identified seven pressing priorities for HBCUs. They include enrollment management, academic quality, infrastructure, federal and state policy, and governance and leadership. HBCUs are also very concerned about their financial viability, from sources of revenue to how they spend their money. At the same time, ensuring student success—their very reason for existence—is a thread throughout the strategic priorities.

"Our hope is that the findings will contribute to the national dialogue about the future of HBCUs and serve as a resource for boards and institutional leaders to focus their important work, now and into the future.[110] In a recent survey conducted by *University Business,* 66 presidents, chancellors, and provosts from institutions across the country weighed in on their higher education priorities for 2016 into 2017. Student success was ranked as the number one

---

[110] Association of Governing Boards of Universities and Colleges. (2014). Top Strategic Issues Facing HBCUs, Now and Into the Future.

priority followed by controlling costs and fundraising.[111] It should be noted that other institutions of higher education need to include 'black minds matter' as a reality and part of their strategic and tactical plans and programming.

"Now let me briefly address a few other concerns such as transportation and apprenticeship opportunities. Transportation systems need to function to get community members to job centers and meet other travel demands, as well as transporting them to school with ease. Transit routes should be user-friendly for buses, motorized vehicles and bicycles. Restructuring the different transit systems will provide jobs and bring opportunities for apprenticeships in trades and arts industries.

"Apprenticeship opportunities can be generated as the community invests in affordable housing for all. There should be a CAPTS program for housing development and neighborhood renewal with affordable housing initiatives. Public housing should be both rental and owner occupied. All neighborhoods should have CAPTS representatives who will assure that their homes are safe, sizable and sanitary for all social and economic levels. Housing acquisition should be flexible and fluid. Affordable housing will be a significant contributor to eradicating the blind mouse of poverty and lead to illumination. No child or family should live in squalor and their ecosystem should help keep them healthy (e.g., no lead). No one should be homeless.

"The community health system should be a CAPTS assisted entity

[111] Education Advisory Board. (2017, January 5). 66 college leaders share their top priorities for 2017. Retrieved from EAB: https://www.eab.com/daily-briefing/2017/01/05/student-success-a-top-priority

to promote mental and physical health services for all residents without racial or other disparities and inequities within treatment, policy, education and advocacy. The system will be user-friendly for individuals experiencing disabilities or health problems and will be an adjunct to their caregivers. It needs to intervene efficaciously with intergenerational trauma and the prevention thereof. Integrated health programs should be funded for critical health conditions (e.g., opioid addiction, suicidality and emotional disorders).

"Black lives matter at all ages and prenatally. There needs to be adequate resources provided for prenatal and infant care. The high mortality for black children should focus on teen parents and their ecosystem. These parents are usually financially fragile. They deserve quality and affordable healthcare.

"As stated earlier, we want to empower the lives of all our black brothers and sisters worldwide by ensuring that every child is trained or educated to work and relate in today's world. We want those who establish businesses to be profitable and return 40% of profits to all employees equally, as well as develop businesses that provide living wages and adequate benefits. Affordable housing and home ownership in safe and sanitary ecosystems are imperative. These goals will be the foci of our next Summit which will be international and Pan-African in scope.

"We all identified many of the same or similar problems, but of paramount importance are the recommendations, programmatic models, resources, etc. that are provided. We need to make sure that we share with our leaders, policy makers and persons of authority the collective knowledge and wisdom that we've gained. Such dialogue is vital to bring about change and help to eliminate the three blind mice: mental illness, miseducation and poverty.

"In closing, on behalf of our host, Mayor Washington, and all of you, I again say thank you. I wish you safe travels back to your homes. May God bless you – and may God bless America!"

Summary

We began this work by looking at the conditions of existence of African people worldwide yesterday and today. We find that African lives, our lives, did not matter as the Creator intended in Genesis I. We used a metaphor, the Three Blind Mice, to describe and explain mental illness, miseducation and poverty from historical, current and emerging perspectives. The first blind mouse is mental illness; the second blind mouse is miseducation; and the third blind mouse is poverty.

Mental Illness. It is extremely difficult to maintain positive mental health when we are born into a world that despises our presence and a world that has instituted barriers to stifle our development as human beings free of traumas that produce and perpetuate depression, anxiety and other mental disorders. Even before we are conceived, conceivers themselves are battling the evils of racism and oppression.

During conceptus, racial disparities exist when our parents access, if they can, prenatal health care. When the child leaves the mother's womb, it encounters a system that makes it very difficult for its parents to nurture and secure the child's ecosystem that is needed for positive human growth and development. There are structures associated with a racist system that prevent African

American children from having a decent roof over their heads and obtaining other basic needs.

Many adolescents are misdiagnosed and mislabeled as mentally ill which prevents them from getting proper mental health care when they need it. Their parents during this time are spending significant time battling the forces of the three blind mice. Inter-generationally, we need to possess full mental health (i.e., wake up every day "in our right minds"). In this psycho-novel, we have provided suggested recommendations to alleviate, if not eradicate, some of the mental illness issues in the black community today.

Miseducation. Miseducation started in Africa and has continued through our enslavement and throughout our emancipation. We must illuminate our minds, eliminate negative propaganda and boldly proclaim who we are. We are heirs of the King - a royal priesthood "fearfully and wonderfully made"! We are from proud and great ancestors. We are from kings and queens who began the history of the world. We are the people who provided the foundation for all that we see good today. We have not been given our due credits for all that we have bestowed upon human kind. After the eradication of our libraries and icons in Africa, we were told that we, as a people, had little or nothing that we gave to society. What a lie!

Our charge now is to dispel this lie, and it is only through illumination of our minds that the transformation will begin. It must be recognized that it is quite difficult for us to be sane in an insane place that tells us that we are less than any other being like ourselves. Therefore, the most sane thing to do is find creative responses to the madness in which we find ourselves embedded.

Poverty. African people were born into a rich heritage. They inherited Africa with all of its riches. For many years African people wanted for nothing until Europeans came to Africa and began to pillage and plunder until they had everything (i.e., resources), and we had nothing. During this grand theft in Africa, we became part of the resources that were being taken; we became an integral part of the Transatlantic Slave Trade and the making of rich white people in America.

Today we can see the economic status of African Americans at the very low end of the economic scale compared to whites. We have yet to receive from them the remuneration for all the work and creativity that we have given to their well-being and financial largesse. Reparations have been constant requests to help make whole the economic vacuum in which we find ourselves.

Without the reparations, blacks have struggled to maintain viable communities with the use of their labor (e.g., sharecropping). Whites have taken many of the factors that provided a viable means of community building and placed them in other parts of the world. Little or none of these resources were placed in Africa. As much as we wanted to work, whites found ways of keeping us "dirt poor, poor and near poor." The plight of many African Americans, especially those in prison, are just as hard today as they were during our enslavement and the first opportunity to get paid for our labor.[112]

---

[112] Impact in Communities, Unity, Pan African Movement, Solidarity with Friends and Allies, Resilience Training

Call to Action

In order for Blacks to eliminate the three blind mice and live in illumination, we must battle on multiple fronts to help energize our communities and help to produce trauma-free and resilient children. Our mission is to form diverse, inclusive and strategic alliances—cooperative partnerships to help institute changes within the wider society. This society includes federal courts, federal agencies, congressional representatives, and executive officials, elected and appointed, who will work in the best interest of social justice for all.

One way that we can advocate social justice is to have educational programming (e.g., the Sesame Street model) to help teach inclusivity and eliminate bigotry. Social justice educational programs can extend to all grade levels and college as well. Federal policies and programs must benefit all Americans and are benign to our brothers and sisters in Africa.

At the state level, we must be just as vigorous in making sure that all government appointees and elected officials are operating policies and programs that are in the best interest of African Americans and other communities. Locally, we must make sure that the CAPTS model is employed with more than a semblance of black community control. We want to recognize and make it possible for all eligible members of the community to vote. In this effort, the black church can play a monumental role because of its capability for outreach and assembly. It is best known for being high on protests and less for seeking prosperity. The black church has a rich history of being a beacon of light and ray of hope for the community. The black church is not only for spiritual growth, it is a place that promotes change and promotes a strong relationship with the Creator and others. It is also a vehicle for socialization of children, and it is available to help meet the needs of the family.

The family is critical for raising children who will be responsible members and leaders in their community. We need to instill in our children at a very young age that black family life and relationships matter. By adolescence, it is advocated that they undergo a Rites of Passage that has an Afrocentric philosophy and a focus on producing strong black youth who value marriage, family and related matters. They will be taught how to acquire and maintain resources that they need to help support themselves, their family and their community.

Black businesses should be a cornerstone of the community, and we must support them. Black businesses need infusions of finances from black banks and other financial institutions. Black businesses should also promote black employment, community engagement and programs. They should be on the cutting edge of helping to eliminate poverty. Central to this goal is establishing a Pan-African business model which brings the best business minds in the diaspora together to help eradicate the blind mouse of poverty.

We should make sure that our communities have adequate parks, libraries, recreational facilities, museums and media centers to help eliminate the miseducation mouse.

We hope that this psycho-novel has enhanced your knowledge and understanding of the three blind mice; given you a toolkit of prescriptions and resources, as well as action plans to help you transform your community and the world around you— going from "darkness to marvelous light."

Hence, ILLUMINATION!

Illumination!

I googled the word illumination
To make sure the definition was right;
I looked it up in Webster's Dictionary
And sure enough it was all about the light!
The Creator said let your light so shine
So to have the right mentality;
It's necessary for us to look to the Creator
Who gives us our spirituality!
A lot of people are walking around
Not realizing that they are ill;
This kind of mental illness
Just can't be cured with a pill.
Miseducation of people
Seems to cause many our problems;
We need to look to the Savior
He's the only one who can solve them!
We walk around in poverty
Like it's really not a big thing;
But if we are led by the spirit
We'd know we serve the King!
The Creator said walk after the spirit
And you won't fulfill the lust of the flesh;
He paved the way for us
Yes, the Creator did it best!
He said He would keep you in perfect peace
If you keep your mind stayed on Him;
The devil wants us to feel defeated
And feel like our situations are grim.
Our Creator doesn't care if you're rich or poor
Or whether you're green, black or white
There are people living in poverty
Our illumination comes from the light!
Mental illness is a disease
And the Creator is an ever present help;
The mind is a terrible thing to waste
So put your trust in Him and no one else!

Belinda Wyche

Bibliography

(n.d.). Retrieved from National Institute of Mental Health: https://www.nimh.nih.gov/index.shtml

"Negro Rule" North Carolina elections. (n.d.). Retrieved from Reddit: https://www.reddit.com/r/PropagandaPosters/comments/2jfir5/negro_rule_north_carolina_elections_1900/

2015 Poverty Guidelines. (2015, September 3). Retrieved from U.S. Department of Health & Human Services: https://aspe.hhs.gov/2015-poverty-guidelines

African American Mental Health. (n.d.). Retrieved from National Alliance on Mental Illness: http://www.nami.org/Find-Support/Diverse-Communities/African-Americans

African Americans in World War II: Fighting for a Double Victory. (n.d.). Retrieved from National WWII Museum: http://www.nationalww2museum.org/assets/pdfs/african-americans-in-world.pdf

African Americans, Impact of the Great Depression on. (n.d.). Retrieved from GALE, U.S. History: http://ic.galegroup.com/ic/uhic/ReferenceDetailsPage/DocumentToolsPortletWindow?displayGroupName=Reference&jsid=7812016b5ea4d6684ea4837e2c6ef921&action=2&catId=&documentId=GALE%7CCX3404500017&u=sand55832&zid=b57acc008e359910d5c24de390bb447b

African-Americans after Reconstruction. (n.d.). Retrieved from Cliffs Notes: https://www.cliffsnotes.com/study-guides/history/us-history-ii/american-society-and-culture-18651900/africanamericans-after-reconstruction

Alcohol Dependence. (n.d.). Retrieved from Allaboutcounseling.com: www.allaboutcounseling.com/library/alcohol-dependence

Anthony T. Browder- Egpyt on the Potomac Field Trip (2014). [Motion Picture].

Anti-Defamation League (ADL). (2013). *10 Ideas for Teaching Black History Month*. Retrieved from ADL: http://www.adl.org/assets/pdf/education-outreach/10-ideas-for-teaching-black-history-month.pdf

Association of Governing Boards of Universities and Colleges. (2014). *Top Strategic Issues Facing HBCUs, Now and Into the Future*.

Audrey Thomas, S. S. (2000). *Racism and Psychiatry*. Citadel.

Basic Statistics. (n.d.). Retrieved from Talk Poverty: https://talkpoverty.org/basics/

Bauman, R. (n.d.). *War on Poverty*. Retrieved from Blackpast.org: http://www.blackpast.org/aah/war-poverty

Bennett, L. (1984). *Before the Mayflower*. Penguin Books.

Bieler, S. (2015, November 24). *Elevating the 2016 Debate: Crime and Justice; What the data really say about race and homicide*. Retrieved from Urban Institute: http://www.urban.org/2016-analysis/what-data-really-say-about-race-and homicide?utm_source=iContact&utm_medium=email&utm_camp aign=Urban%20Institute%20Update&utm_content=w%2Fo+ima ge+-+Urban+Institute+Update+-+12%2F03%2F2015

Browder, A. T. (2017, March 1). *Egypt on the Potomac Field Trip*. Retrieved from YouTube: https://www.youtube.com/watch?v=SXCafoGpZ9M

Caricatures of African Americans: The Brute. (2012, November 25). Retrieved from Authentic History Center: http://www.authentichistory.com/diversity/african/4-brute/

Charles Murray. (n.d.). Retrieved from Southern Poverty Law Center: https://www.splcenter.org/fighting-hate/extremist-files/individual/charles-murray

Charles, M. (2013, December 22). *Author Interview: Dr. Frances Cress Welsing*. Retrieved from Knowshi: http://knowshi.com/author-interview-dr-frances-cress-welsing/

Chigozie, E. (n.d.). *5 Most Powerful African Kings From History.* Retrieved from Answers Africa: http://answersafrica.com/african-kings.html

Definition of Poverty. (n.d.). Retrieved from Merrian-Webster: http://www.merriam-webster.com/dictionary/poverty

DeGruy, J. (2005). *Posttraumatic Slave Syndrome.* Joy DeGruy Publications, Inc.

Dewbury, A. (2007). The American School and Scientific Racism in Early American Anthropology. *Histories of Anthropology Annual,* 142.

Edelman, P. (2012, June 22). *The State of Poverty in America.* Retrieved from The American Prospect: http://prospect.org/article/state-poverty-america

Education Advisory Board. (2017, January 5). *66 college leaders share their top priorities for 2017.* Retrieved from EAB: https://www.eab.com/daily-briefing/2017/01/05/student-success-a-top-priority

Exodusters: Black Migration to Kansas after Reconstruction. (n.d.). Retrieved from Geni: https://www.geni.com/projects/Exodusters-Black-Migration-to-Kansas-after-Reconstruction/9276

Farbota, K. (2016, September 2). *Black Crime Rates: What Happens When Numbers Aren't Neutral.* Retrieved from The Huffington Post: http://www.huffingtonpost.com/kim-farbota/black-crime-rates-your-st_b_8078586.html

Fisher, G. (1992). *The Development and History of the Poverty Thresholds.* Retrieved from Social Security Bulletin: https://www.ssa.gov/history/fisheronpoverty.html

From Slave Labor to Free Labor. (2003). Retrieved from Digital History: http://www.digitalhistory.uh.edu/exhibits/reconstruction/section3/section3_intro.html

Fruits of Reconstruction. (n.d.). Retrieved from African American Odyssey: https://memory.loc.gov/ammem/aaohtml/exhibit/aopart5b.html

Gilens, M. (2003). *How the Poor Became Black: The Racialization of American Poverty in the Mass Media.* Retrieved from The University of Michigan: https://www.press.umich.edu/pdf/9780472068319-ch4.pdf

Gordon, T. (2015, January 23). *10 Pieces of Evidence That Prove Black People Sailed to the Americas Long Before Columbus.* Retrieved from Atlanta Black Star: http://atlantablackstar.com/2015/01/23/10-pieces-of-evidence-that-prove-black-people-sailed-to-the-americas-long-before-columbus/

Graves, D. (n.d.). *Wormley Hotel.* Retrieved from The White House Historical Association: https://www.whitehousehistory.org/wormley-hotel-1

Hamblet, W. (2009, November 12). *'Civilisation' and the myth of African 'savagery'.* Retrieved from Pambazuka News: http://www.pambazuka.org/governance/%E2%80%98civilisation%E2%80%99-and-myth-african-%E2%80%98savagery%E2%80%99

Henry Louis Gates, J. (n.d.). *Did African-American Slaves Rebel?* Retrieved from WHRO: http://www.pbs.org/wnet/african-americans-many-rivers-to-cross/history/did-african-american-slaves-rebel/

History. (n.d.). Retrieved from Lonely Planet: http://www.lonelyplanet.com/africa/history

History of Slavery in America. (n.d.). Retrieved from Open Computing Facility, Berkeley University: https://www.ocf.berkeley.edu/~arihuang/academic/abg/slavery/history.html

Hodges, K. (n.d.). *Continuity or Change: African Americans in World War II.* Retrieved from UMBC: http://www.umbc.edu/che/tahlessons/pdf/Continuity_or_Change_African_Americans_in_World_War_II(PrinterFriendly).pdf

How is poverty measured in the United States? (2016, September 13). Retrieved from Center for Poverty Research:

http://poverty.ucdavis.edu/faq/how-poverty-measured-united-states

Imhotep. (n.d.). Retrieved from BBC:
http://www.bbc.co.uk/history/historic_figures/imhotep.shtml

Isserman, M. (2012). *50 Years Later: Poverty and The Other America.* Retrieved from Dissent Magazine:
https://www.dissentmagazine.org/article/50-years-later-poverty-and-the-other-america

Johnson, L. B. (1964, January 8). *Annual Message to the Congress on the State of the Union.* Retrieved from The American Presidency Project:
http://www.presidency.ucsb.edu/ws/?pid=26787

Jr., H. L. (n.d.). *What Was Black America's Double War?* Retrieved from WHRO: http://www.pbs.org/wnet/african-americans-many-rivers-to-cross/history/what-was-black-americas-double-war/

Lauter, D. (2016, August 14). *How do Americans view poverty? Many blue-collar whites, key to Trump, criticize poor people as lazy and content to stay on welfare.* Retrieved from LA Times:
http://www.latimes.com/projects/la-na-pol-poverty-poll/

Mark, J. (2016, February 16). *Imhotep.* Retrieved from Ancient History Encyclopedia: http://www.ancient.eu/imhotep/

Matthews, D. (2014, January 8). *Everything you need to know about the war on poverty.* Retrieved from Washington Post:
https://www.washingtonpost.com/news/wonk/wp/2014/01/08/everything-you-need-to-know-about-the-war-on-poverty/

Mental Health and African Americans. (n.d.). Retrieved from U.S. Department of Health and Human Services Office of Minority Health:
http://minorityhealth.hhs.gov/omh/browse.aspx?lvl=4&lvlID=24

Mental Health and Substance Use Disorders. (n.d.). Retrieved from U.S. Department of Health & Human Services:
https://www.mentalhealth.gov/what-to-look-for/substance-abuse/index.html

Mihm, S. (2014, August 24). *Where slavrey thrived, inequality rules today.*
Retrieved from Boston Globe:
https://www.bostonglobe.com/ideas/2014/08/23/where-slavery-
thrived-inequality-rules-
today/iF5zgFsXncPoYmYCMMs67J/story.html

Minnesota, T. U. (n.d.). *Why is Spirituality Important?* Retrieved from Taking
Charge of Your Health & Well-Being:
https://www.takingcharge.csh.umn.edu/enhance-your-
wellbeing/purpose/spirituality/why-spirituality-important

Mitchell, J. (2015, October 23). *God Over Everything: Black Spirituality and the
Paradox of Religion.* Retrieved from Huffington Post:
http://www.huffingtonpost.com/Julian-mitchell/god- over-
everything-

Morgan, J. (2016). *Review: Black Rage.* Retrieved from Culture + Youth
Studies: http://cultureandyouth.org/african-american-
culture/books-african-american-culture/black-rage/

National League of Cities. (2016, Decemnber 8). *State of the Cities 2016.*
Retrieved from National League of Cities:
http://www.nic.org/resource/state-of-the-cities-2016

Omar Reid, S. M. (2004). *Posttraumatic Slavery Disorder.* Xlibris.

Owen, J. (2007, July 18). *National Geographic News.* Retrieved from National
Geographic:
http://news.nationalgeographic.com/news/2007/07/070718-
african-origin.html

Painter, N. I. (2006, February 14). *Slavery: A Dehumanizing Institution.*
Retrieved from OUPblog:
http://blog.oup.com/2006/02/slavery_a_dehum/

Parker, J. (n.d.). *"What is Poverty?".* Retrieved from Michigan State
University: https://msu.edu/~jdowell/135/JGParker.html

Pasha. (2007, October 5). *Henry Boyd- Black inventor.* Retrieved from Each
One Teach One: http://www.eachoneteachone.org.uk/henry-
boyd/

Reconstruction. (n.d.). Retrieved from History.com:
  http://www.history.com/topics/american-civil-war/reconstruction

Reconstruction and Its Aftermath. (n.d.). Retrieved from African American
  Odyssey:
  https://memory.loc.gov/ammem/aaohtml/exhibit/aopart5.html

Reconstruction, America's First Attempt to Integrate. (n.d.). Retrieved from
  African American Registry:
  http://www.aaregistry.org/historic_events/view/reconstruction-
  americas-first-attempt-integrate

Sachsen-Gotha, S. (2014, November 24). *10 Racist Scientific Theories that
  Changed the World.* Retrieved from Listverse:
  http://listverse.com/2014/11/24/ten-racist-scientific-theories-
  that-changed-the-world/

Savali, K. (2015, June 2). *Throw Away the Script: How Media Bias Is Killing
  Black America.* Retrieved from The Root:
  http://www.theroot.com/articles/culture/2015/06/how_media_b
  ias_is_killing_black_america/

Savvy Sista. (2007). *African Queens: Candace- Empress of Ethiopia (332 B.C.).*
  Retrieved from The Savvy Sista:
  http://www.thesavvysista.com/2007/10/african-queens-candace-
  empress-of.html

Schwartzapfel, B. a. (2015, May 13). *Willie Horton Revisited.* Retrieved from
  The Marshall Project:
  https://www.themarshallproject.org/2015/05/13/willie-horton-
  revisited#.I67bCOjkC

Scott, T. (2014, December 26). *10 Racist Scientific Theories About Black People
  That Have Been Thoroughly Debunked.* Retrieved from Atlanta Black
  Star: http://atlantablackstar.com/2014/12/26/10-racist-scientific-
  theories-about-black-people-that-has-been-thoroughly-debunked/

Sharecropping. (n.d.). Retrieved from History.com:
  http://www.history.com/topics/black-history/sharecropping

Smith, V. (n.d.). *Excerpts from Slave Narratives*. Retrieved from UNESCO
ASPnet TST: http://www.vgskole.net/prosjekt/slavrute/4.htm

*Social Science Literature Review: Media Representations and Impact on the Lives of
Black Men and Boys*. (2011, October). Retrieved from The
Opportunity Agenda:
http://www.racialequitytools.org/resourcefiles/Media-Impact-
onLives-of-Black-Men-and-Boys-OppAgenda.pdf

Staff, M. C. (2015, October 15). *Definition*. Retrieved from Mayo Clinic:
http://www.mayoclinic.org/diseases-conditions/mental-
illness/basics/definition/con-20033813

Substance Use Disorders. (2015, October 27). Retrieved from Substance Abuse
and Mental Health Services Administration:
http://www.samhsa.gov/disorders/substance-use

Sustar, L. (2012, June 28). *Blacks and the Great Depression*. Retrieved from
SocialistWorker.org:
http://socialistworker.org/2012/06/28/blacks-and-the-great-
depression

Talbot, A. (2013, May 7). *Debunking the IQ Myth*. Retrieved from American
Renaissance: http://www.amren.com/news/2013/05/debunking-
the-iq-myth/

Taylor, C. (n.d.). *Patriotism Crosses the Color Line: African Americans in World
War II*. Retrieved from The Gilder Lehrman Institute of American
History: https://www.gilderlehrman.org/history-by-era/world-
war-ii/essays/patriotism-crosses-color-line-african-americans-
world-war-ii

The Booker T. Washington Era. (n.d.). Retrieved from African American
Odyssey:
https://memory.loc.gov/ammem/aaohtml/exhibit/aopart6.html

The Great Depression. (n.d.). Retrieved from Amistad Digital Resource:
http://www.amistadresource.org/plantation_to_ghetto/the_great_
depression.html

Thernstrom, A. a. (1998, March 1). *Black Progress; How far we've come, and how*

far we have to go. Retrieved from Brookings:
https://www.brookings.edu/articles/black-progress-how-far-weve-come-and-how-far-we-have-to-go/

Tracy. (2014, February 11). *5 Inventions by Enslaved Black Men Blocked by US Patent Office*. Retrieved from Atlanta Black Star:
http://atlantablackstar.com/2014/02/11/5-inventions-by-enslaved-black-men-blocked-by-us-patent-office/3/

U.S. Department of Justice. (2014). *Expanded Homicide Date Table 6.*
Retrieved from FBI:UCR: https://ucr.fbi.gov/crime-in-the-u.s/2014/crime-in-the-u.s.-2014/tables/expanded-homicide-data/expanded_homicide_data_table_6_murder_race_and_sex_of_vicitm_by_race_and_sex_of_offender_2014.xls

United States Census Bureau. (2013). *American Fact Finder.* Retrieved from United States Census Bureau:
https://factfinder.census.gov/faces/tableservices/jsf/pages/produ ctview.xhtml?src=bkmk

University of Minnesota. (n.d.). *Seven Spiritual Needs.* Retrieved from Taking Charge of Your Health & Well-Being:
https://www.takingcharge.csh.umn.edu/enhance-your-wellbeing/purpose/spirituality/seven-spiritual-needs

University of Minnesota. (n.d.). *What is Spirituality?* Retrieved from Taking Charge of Your Health and Well-Being:
https://www.takingcharge.csh.umn.edu/what-spirituality

Wade, L. (2016, July 8). *European Neandertals were cannibals.* Retrieved from Science: http://www.sciencemag.org/news/2016/07/european-neandertals-were-cannibals

Welsing, D. F. (2013, September 3). *Surviving Racism in the 21st Century- Part I.*
Retrieved from YouTube:
https://www.youtube.com/watch?v=Zdblpa0AfuQ

What causes depression? (n.d.). Retrieved from Beyond Blue:
https://www.beyondblue.org.au/the-facts/depression/what-causes-depression

What is poverty? (n.d.). Retrieved from Economic and Social Inclusion
    Corporation:
    http://www2.gnb.ca/content/gnb/en/departments/esic/overview
    /content/what_is_poverty.html

Wyse, E. (n.d.). *The History of "Great is Thy Faithfulness"*. Retrieved from
    LifeWay: http://m.lifeway.com/Article/the-history-of-Great-Is-
    Thy-Faithfulness

Resource Directory

Additional information can be obtained from government agencies, nonprofit organizations, websites, books and articles. Contact information is provided.

MENTAL HEALTH

Organizations

American Psychiatric Association
1000 Wilson Boulevard, Suite 1825
Arlington, VA 22209
Phone: 703-907-7300
Website: http://psychiatry.org

American Psychological Association
750 First Street, NE
Washington, DC 20002
Phone: 800-374-2721
Website: http://www.apa.org

Anxiety.org
4600 Campus Drive, Suite 107
Newport Beach, CA 92660
Phone: 949-267-4117
Website: http://www.anxiety.org

Anxiety and Depression Association of America
8701 Georgia Ave., Suite 412
Silver Spring, MD 20910
Phone: 240-485-1001
Website: https://www.adaa.org

Association of Black Psychologists
7119 Allentown Road, Suite 203
Fort Washington, MD 20744-1521
Phone: 301-449-3082
Website: http://abpsi@abpsi.org

Black Organizing for Leadership and Dignity
1001 Connecticut Ave., NW, Suite 201
Washington, DC 20036
Phone: 305-590-8224
Website: http://boldorganizing.org

Black Organizing Project
1035 W Grand Ave
Oakland, CA 98607

Phone: 510-891-1219
Website: http://blackorganizingproject.org

Domestic Violence & Child Advocacy Center
P.O. Box 5466
Cleveland, OH 44101
Phone: 216-229-2420
Website: http://www.dvcac.org

Freedom From Fear
308 Seaview Avenue
Staten Island, NY 10305
Phone: 718-351-1717
Website: http://www.freedomfromfear.org

Institute on Domestic Violence in the African American Community
1404 Gortner Avenue
Saint Paul, MN 55108
Phone: 877-643-8222
Website: http://www.idvaac.org

National Alliance on Mental Illness
3830 N. Fairfax Drive, Suite 100
Arlington, VA 22203
Phone: 703-524-7600
Website: http://www.nami.org

The Association for Addiction Professionals
44 Canal Center Plaza, Suite 301
Alexandria, VA 22314
Phone: 800-548-0497
Website: http://www.naadac.org

The Satcher Health Leadership Institute
720 Westview Drive SW
Atlanta, GA 30310
Phone: 404-756-8914
Website: http://www.communityvoices.org

Voices of Our Nation Arts Foundation
740 River Road
Fair Haven, NJ 07704
Website: http://www.vonacommunity.org

Websites

7 Statistics You Need to Know about Black-On-Black Crime
http://www.dailywire.com/news/7441/7-statistics-you-need-know-about-black-black-crime-aaron-bandler

African American Community Mental Health
http://www.dbhds.virginia.gov/library/cultural%20and%20linguistic%20competence/provider%20material/diverse/africanamerican_mentalhealth_factsheet_2009.pdf

African American Mental Illness Stigma
http://www.huffingtonpost.com/news/african-americans-mental-illness-stigma/ty

African-American Youth and Exposure to Community Violence
http://www.psysr.org/jsacp/Thomas-v4n1-12_54-68.pdf

Atlanta Black Star
http://atlantablackstar.com/2015/07/03/ptsd-and-mental-health-disorders-in-black-people-linked-to-trauma-from-racism-and-violence/

Black America's Invisible Crime
http://www.essence.com/2014/09/05/propublica-post-traumatic-stress-disorder

Criminal Justice Fact Sheet
http://www.naacp.org/criminal-justice-fact-sheet/

Domestic Violence among African Americans
http://criminal-justice.iresearchnet.com/crime/domestic-violence/african-americans/

Domestic Violence in the African American Community
http://pluralism.org/wp-content/uploads/2015/08/Jordan.pdf

Domestic Violence in the African American Community: An Analysis of Social and Structural Factors
https://www.researchgate.net/publication/249675629_Domestic_Violence_in_the_African_American_Community_An_Analysis_of_Social_and_Structural_Factors

How Gang Violence is Tearing Black America Apart
http://thegrio.com/2012/07/27/how-gang-violence-is-tearing-black-america-apart/

How the War on Drugs Fails Black Communities
http://reason.com/archives/2016/07/14/how-the-war-on-drugs-fails-black-communities

Mapping Police Violence
https://mappingpoliceviolence.org

Mental Health America
http://www.mentalhealthamerica.net/african-american-mental-health

Mental Health in the African American
http://www.cpp.edu/~healthcounseling/Documents/africanamer-final-1-15-09.pdf

Journalist's Resources
https://journalistsresource.org/studies/society/race-society/police-violence-black-communities-emergency-calls

The Severely Distressed African American Family in the Crack Era
https://www.ncbi.nlm.nih.gov/pmc/articles/PMC2565489/

Vice
https://www.vice.com/en_us/article/the-ripple-effects-of-police-violence-253

Violence and the African-American Community
https://academic.udayton.edu/health/01status/98chipma.htm

Books

Boyd, Herb. Race and Resistance ; African-Americans in the Twenty-first Century. Cambridge, MA: South End, 2002.

Hampton, Robert L., Thomas P. Gullotta, and Raymond L. Crowel. Handbook of African American Health. New York: Guilford, 2010.

Hastings, Julia F., and Pamela P. Martin. African Americans and Depression: Signs, Awareness, Treatments, and Interventions. Lanham: Rowman & Littlefield, 2015.

Head, John. Black Men and Depression: Understanding and Overcoming Depression in Black Men. New York: Harlem Moon/Broadway, 2005.
Kennedy, David M. Don't Shoot: One Man, a Street Fellowship, and the End of

Violence in Inner-city America. New York: Bloomsbury USA, 2011.

Hooks, Bell. Rock My Soul: Black People and Self-esteem. New York: Atria, 2003.

Hooks, Bell. "Sisters of the Yam: Black Women and Self-Recovery / Edition 2." Barnes & Noble. South End Press, n.d. Web. 03 Feb. 2017.

Humann, Heather Duerre. Domestic Abuse in the Novels of African American Women: A Critical Study. Jefferson, NC: McFarland &,, 2014. Print.

James, William H., and Stephen L. Johnson. Doin' Drugs: Patterns of African American Addiction. Austin: U of Texas, 1996.

Johnson, Ruth W. African American Voices: African American Health Educators Speak out. New York: National League for Nursing, 1995.

Leap, Jorja. Jumped In: What Gangs Taught Me about Violence, Drugs, Love, and Redemption. Boston: Beacon, 2012.

Logan, Sadye Louise, and Edith M. Freeman. Health Care in the Black Community: Empowerment, Knowledge, Skills, and Collectivism. New York: Haworth, 2000.

Miller, Jody. Getting Played: African American Girls, Urban Inequality, and Gendered Violence. New York: New York UP, 2008.

Murray, Kennard. Shackled by a Heavy Burden: An Examination of Barriers Pastors Face When Providing Pastoral Counseling or Referrals in the African American Church. Eugene, Or.: Resource Publications, 2011.

Parham, Thomas A., Adisa Ajamu, Joseph L. White, and Roslyn Caldwell. The Psychology of Blacks: Centering Our Perspectives in the African Consciousness. Boston: Prentice Hall, 2011.

Roberts, Kevin D. African American Issues. Westport, CT: Greenwood, 2006.

Sanders, Mark. Substance Use Disorders in African American Communities: Prevention, Treatment and Recovery. London: Routledge, 2014.

Williams, Terrie M. Black Pain: It Just Looks Like We're Not Hurting Paperback – January 6, 2009.

Williams, Stephen. The Malignant Ideology: Exploring the Connection between Black History and Gang Violence. Bloomington, IN: Xlibris, 2012.

MISEDUCATION

Websites

History is a weapon
http://www.historyisaweapon.com/defcon1/misedne.html

The Mis-Education of the Reformed Negro
http://www.reformedblacksofamerica.org/blog1/index.php?itemid=300

Q&A: The Mis-Education Of African-American Girls
http://www.npr.org/sections/ed/2014/09/25/351186785/q-a-the-mis-education-of-african-american-girls

Fixing the Miseducation of Black Children
http://www.theroot.com/fixing-the-miseducation-of-black-children-1790897230

Reunion Black Family
http://www.reunionblackfamily.com/apps/blog/show/44001614-how-black- people-have-been-miseducated-to-serve-the-agenda-s-of-the-ruling-white-elites-

Books

Asante, Molefi Kete. African Pyramids of Knowledge: Kemet, Afrocentricity and Africology. Brooklyn, NY: Universal Write Publications LLC, 2015.

DuBoise, W.E.B. The Soul of Black Folk. N.p.: Quiet Vision Pub,

2008. Fage, J. D. A History of Africa. New York: Knopf, 1978.

Fanon, Frantz. Black Skin, White Masks. New York: Grove, 1967.

Foner, Philip Sheldon. History of Black Americans. Westport, Conn. U.a.: Greenwood, 1983.

Franklin, John Hope. From Slavery to Freedom: A History of Negro Americans. New York: Knopf, 1967.

Griffin, John Howard. Black Like Me. Boston: Houghton Mifflin, 1977.

Karenga, Maulana. Introduction to Black Studies. Los Angeles: U of Sankore, 1993.

Karenga, Maulana. Race, Ethnicity and Multiculturalism: Issues in Domination Resistance and Diversity. University of Sankore Press.: n.p., n.d.

Karenga, Maulana. The Million Man March, Day of Absence: Mission Statement. Washington, D.C.: Published for the National Million Man March/Day of Absence, Organizing Committee, 1995.

Klarman, Michael J. Unfinished Business: Racial Equality in American History. Oxford: Oxford UP, 2007.

Lerone Bennett Jr. "Before the Mayflower." Google Books. N.p., n.d. Web. 04 Feb. 2017.

Stewart, Jeffrey C. 1001 Things Everyone Should Know about African-American History. New York: Doubleday, 1996.

Wright, W. D. Black History and Black Identity: A Call for a New Historiography. Westport, CT: Praeger, 2002.

POVERTY

Websites

African American Poverty: Concentrated and Multi-Generational
http://www.epi.org/blog/african-american-poverty-concentrated-multi/

Being Poor, Black and American
http://www.aft.org/sites/default/files/periodicals/Wilson.pdf

Causes and Effects of Poverty
https://www.cliffsnotes.com/study-guides/sociology/social-and-global-stratification/causes-and-effects-of-poverty

LBJ's "War on Poverty" Hurt Black Americans
http://www.nationalcenter.org/P21PR-WarOnPoverty_010814.html

Portrait of Inequality 2011 Black Children in America
http://www.childrensdefense.org/campaigns/black-community-crusade-for-children-II/bccc-assets/portrait-of-inequality.pdf

Poverty leads to death for more black Americans than whites
https://www.theguardian.com/money/us-money-blog/2015/jan/05/rising-income-inequality-deadlier-for-black-americans-study

Racism Causes Poverty
http://ic.galegroup.com/ic/ovic/ViewpointsDetailsPage/DocumentToolsPortletWindow?displayGroupName=Viewpoints&jsid=732dfd18cf9230a16181221b1dd06881&action=2&catId=&documentId=GALE%7CEJ3010159279&u=oak30216&zid=d69f8c2dcb2375a6963eeaa4eda9253e

The Culture of Poverty and its Effect on African Americans in Urban America
https://pages.shanti.virginia.edu/Morgan_McCabe_3/2015/04/28/the-culture-of-poverty-and-its-effect-on-african-americans-in-urban-america/

Three lessons about black poverty
http://www.epi.org/publication/the_lessons_of_black_poverty/

The Impact of Poverty on African American Children in the Child Welfare and Juvenile Justice Systems
http://files.eric.ed.gov/fulltext/EJ913052.pdf

Books

Danziger, Sheldon, and Ann Chih. Lin. Coping with Poverty: The Social Contexts of Neighborhood, Work, and Family in the African-American Community. Ann Arbor: U of Michigan, 2000.

Franklin, Robert Michael. Crisis in the Village: Restoring Hope in African American Communities. Minneapolis: Fortress, 2007.

Martin, Lori Latrice. Black Asset Poverty and the Enduring Racial Divide. Boulder, CO: FirstForumPress, 2013.

Orleck, Annelise, and Lisa Gayle Hazirjian. The War on Poverty: A New Grassroots History, 1964-1980. Athens: U of Georgia, 2011.

Paris, Peter J. Religion and Poverty: Pan-African Perspectives. Durham: Duke UP, 2009.

Polednak, Anthony P. Segregation, Poverty, and Mortality in Urban African Americans. New York: Oxford UP, 1997.

Stack, Carol B. All Our Kin: Strategies for Survival in a Black Community. New York: Harper & Row, 1974.

About the Authors

Dr. James E. Savage, Jr.

Dr. James E. Savage, Jr. is a clinical psychologist and the Founder and C.E.O. of the Institute for Life Enrichment, freestanding mental health clinics based in Washington, D.C., and two locations in Maryland. With decades of experience in academia and private practice, Dr. Savage and the Institute were among the first to promote and provide a black mental health presence in the Washington Metropolitan Area. Combined with his extensive leadership experience, he is a proven force and a heeded voice in the field of black psychology.

Dr. Savage has demonstrated great leadership by serving as Chair of the District of Columbia Board of Psychology, President of the D.C. Chapter of the Association of Black Psychologists, the 37th President of the Association of Black Psychologists, President of the D.C. Psychological Association and a longstanding, viable member of the International Transactional Analysis Association and American Psychological Association.

Dr. Catherine I. Williams

Dr. Catherine I. Williams is CEO of Strategic Training, Empowerment Programming and Solutions (STEPS, LLC), a private global consulting firm which provides diverse training and development services to public and private sector organizations. She is also owner of STEPS Publishing. Her areas of expertise include coalition building, community development and public administration. She is an educator, administrator, training specialist and author who has received numerous awards for community development, leadership and youth empowerment programs.

Among her many publications are Succexcellence: Reaching Success and Excellence, Succexcellence God's Way, Christian Success Initiatives, The "U Factor" for Success, Steps for Effective Writing, and numerous training books and manuals. Some of her workshops include: Leadership Imperatives; Community Economic Development; Strategic Planning; Inside and Outside the Walls of the Church; Youth Employment and Training; and Maximizing Potential for Growth.

www.ingramcontent.com/pod-product-compliance
Lightning Source LLC
Chambersburg PA
CBHW070337260626
47160CB00003B/1074